D0821531

Against God

Against God

Patrick Senécal

translated by
Susan Ouriou and Christelle Morelli

QUATTRO BOOKS

The publication of *Against God* has been generously supported by the Canada Council for the Arts and the Ontario Arts Council.

Cover design: Julie McNeill
Typography: Grey Wolf Typography

Library and Archives Canada Cataloguing in Publication

Senécal, Patrick
[Contre Dieu. English]
    Against God / Patrick Senécal; translated by Susan Ouriou.

Translation of: Contre Dieu.
Also issued in electronic format.
ISBN 978-1-926802-78-7

    I. Ouriou, Susan II. Title. III. Title: Contre
Dieu. English.

PS8587.E544C6513 2012   C843'.54   C2012-900243-7

Published by Quattro Books Inc.
89 Pinewood Avenue
Toronto, Ontario, M6C 2V2
www.quattrobooks.ca

Printed in Canada

- *We had a really good day.*

- *Great. How's your mom?*

- *Happy and healthy. Frankly, she amazes me. She says to say hi.*

- *Tell her hi back. Are you leaving soon?*

- *We'll have our coats on in a minute or two. It's not snowing, we should be home within an hour. Have you had supper yet?*

- *Just finished. I heated up some tourtière.*

- *Always the gourmet! What about the store?*

- *For such a sunny Sunday, we did well. Everyone was out buying skis, I'm not sure why. But I'm not complaining. (laughter) Looks like we'll be spending three weeks in Florida next fall 'stead of just two.*

- Really?

- See what a good idea it is for me to work on a Sunday every once in a while!

- As if your staff can't manage without you!

- I'm indispensable, you know that.

- (laughter) Uh-huh. Hey, the kids want to talk to you.

- Put them on.

- Hi, Daddy.

- Hi, sweetheart. Were you good for Grandma?

- Yup. She gave us lots of chocolates. And money for my piggy bank. Four loonies 'cause I'm 4.

- Lucky you, eh?

- I love you, Daddy. I can't wait to see you.

- I love you, too.

- Here's Alexis.

- Hewo, Daddy . . .

- Hey champ. Were you good for Grandma, too?

- Yeth . . .

- I hear she gave you candy.

- Yeth . . . loth.

- Did you save any for me?

- Uh-uh. I eated it all.

- You candy-monster! I love you, little man.

- Wuv you, Daddy.

- Can you put Mommy on?

- Okay, we're off. How 'bout a movie we can cuddle to tonight?

- Good idea. Stop in at the movie store.

- Okay. I can't wait to see you.

- Me too.

and it all starts when you go to the front door only to be confronted with two cops who look at you as though they're carrying the weight of the world on their shoulders, they ask you your name and your answer doesn't make them feel any better, their faces just get even longer, so you wait, your left hand on the doorknob, your right holding onto the TV remote, and finally you ask what's going on, they ask if you're married to Judith Péloquin, and your voice is louder now, your voice is shaking now as you repeat your

- Christ, what's this all about?

question, then one of the two finally dares look you in the eye, he explains, you listen, at first incredulous, then frightened, next in denial, of course, your old standby whenever you're confronted with something you don't want to accept, and you say that's impossible, and you say that you spoke to them an hour ago, and you hammer at him in the tone of someone who will brook no opposition, but the officer states they were discovered about thirty minutes ago, you're still in denial, you cry "no" several times, you even try to close the door on them but they stop you, they enter, gently they try to calm you, but you walk away, you pace the room, you yell that there's been a mistake, you notice you are still holding the remote, the TV is still playing the sports DVD you were watching with such pleasure a short five minutes ago, and suddenly your legs won't hold you anymore, suddenly you collapse, you fall, you drop to your knees, your sobs, your cries, your hands pull at your hair, and all you remember of the officers' verbiage is the last part, that you must identify the bodies, you spring to your feet, yes, you absolutely have to see them, now, right now, and you climb into the cop car, you drive to the hospital, but when they show you Judith's body, your frenzy dissolves, turns into bitter futile tendrils dispersing through the universe, and when you recognize Béatrice you start to cry again, but you don't recognize the third body, it belongs to a boy of two or so but how to tell whether this is Alexis, the face too disfigured, too destroyed, but then you notice the birthmark on his left thigh and from that point on you founder into such hysteria, such confusion that they have to inject you with a tranquilizer that plunges you into a night's long sleep, then you wake up in a strange bed in a hospital room, you turn your head and see Jean-Marc, Judith's older brother, his tie undone, his features haggard, he notices that you're awake, draws near, hugs you, you both cry for a moment, but you want to understand, to know more, you ask for explanations, so Jean-Marc tells you painfully, with frequent interruptions to blow his nose, to regain control of his trembling voice, but you grasp the main thrust, Judith's car fell into a ravine off that damn winding road you've taken so often, in the hairpin curve that you know so well, the car rolled several times as it fell before hitting a stone wall below, was it Judith who missed the curve, or a car coming from the opposite direction that took the curve too wide and forced your wife to veer off the road, the cops don't know, but they're leaning toward the first hypothesis, there was after all a sheer layer of ice on the road and if another car was involved, most likely it would have stopped, but there's no way of knowing, the police are investigating in any case, but you stop listening, your head turned to the window, your gaze bewildered, and you mumble that you don't have it in you to look after the formalities, funerals, all of it, you're simply incapable, and you burst into tears saying you'll never be able to, it's too much, too too much, and Jean-Marc takes your arm, Jean-Marc tells you he'll look after everything, Jean-Marc always so generous, so helpful, and you observe him for a moment perplexed, you turn away, your gaze unfocused and distant, silence, green walls, a voice over the intercom, coughing in the hallways, and when finally you speak

- I want the funerals held soon. Before the weekend. As soon as possible.

you're still looking out the window, Jean-Marc nods, enfolds you in his arms again and you let him, finally he leaves, you're alone, you do nothing, absolutely nothing, an hour later you leave the hospital but are surprised to see some seven or eight people approaching, cameras, tape recorders at the ready, journalists eager for comments, holding out their mics to you like so many poisoned lollipops, and you're taken aback, you lengthen your stride, say no comment, your voice calm, your eyes evasive, but they follow you to the taxi as you climb in and repeat the same words, the restraint in your voice is surprising but I'm sure that inside, you're seething, calm was never a notable virtue of yours, but you hold yourself together, the taxi takes off, you don't move, just massage your face ever so slowly, twenty minutes, stop, get out, you walk to the front door of your house but you stop short, but you observe it closely, but you scrutinize the house, dread in your eyes, you rummage through your pockets, your keys are there, so you slide into your car and start it up, you drive toward the City, the clock on the dash reads ten forty, you reach the north bridge in under thirty minutes, you cross over, skyscrapers piercing the sky in the distance, the busy streets, pedestrians everywhere, finally you stop in a neighbourhood full of duplexes and triplexes, climb the stairs to a duplex, ring a doorbell, two long minutes, the door opens, Sylvain still half-asleep, his thick black curly hair all dishevelled, surprised to see you, he laughs as he says something big must be up for you to drop by on a Monday morning, but at last your zombie eyes straight out of one of the old horror movies you loved to watch as teens register with him, he asks you to wait a minute then, disappears, two minutes, a pretty young girl appears, twenty-five or so, shoots you a dirty look, walks past and down the sidewalk, then Sylvain returns, invites you to come inside, have a seat, but you can't wait to be inside, you

    - They're all dead, Sylvain.

           tell him now, on the doorstep, but clearly he doesn't understand, his brow knit, his head turned slightly to the right, you sob then and, now, yes, he understands, the horror, the unthinkable, the impossible, he grabs you, pulls you inside, you let him, you're shaking all over, you both stand in the living room and cry together, in each other's arms, two ruins leaning on each other so as not to crumble, then come the questions, your confused and fragmented explanations, lacerated with sobs and cries, Sylvain calls the record store he works for and tells them he won't be in that afternoon, he even tells the person protesting on the other end to go to hell, but you object, point out that he could be fired, but Sylvain doesn't give a damn, Sylvain reminds you he never keeps a job for more than six months, he brings out a bottle of scotch, two drinks downed in a matter of seconds followed by two more, and in no time the apartment becomes the scene of your communion in rage, despair and incomprehension, and there's a phrase you repeat

    - Where'd I go wrong?

                three or four times, unable to stop eyeing your friend's modest one-bedroom apartment and its decor, a couple of nondescript laminated posters on the walls, an old TV and antique stereo, walls yellow with cigarette smoke, Sylvain finally notices your gaze, asks you what's wrong, but your answer

    - It's so different . . . So different . . .

              is obscure, Sylvain asks different from what, but suddenly you call Guy on your cell phone, tell him you won't be in to the store today, he'll have to place the orders himself, you don't give a reason and you hang up, stare hard at your cell phone mumbling that you've only missed four weekdays of work since your store opened six years ago, Sylvain thinks you're a fool to worry about stuff like that, and another quick round, and your friend decrees you'll sleep there tonight, your friend swears he won't leave you alone for a minute, your friend starts to cry again, but you refuse, it makes no sense, you don't want to disrupt his life, his routine, but he waves you off with a

    - C'mon, what routine? Shit, make the most of it; for once my lack of organization is good for something!

broad gesture, and you look hard at him in livid bafflement, struck by his words, then you spring to your feet, agitated, you have to go, Sylvain can't believe his ears, he orders you to stay put, but no, you can't, so Sylvain runs to his room, says he'll get dressed and go with you, but you yell that you'll call him tonight, it's a promise, and you're already outside, half-running to your car, you slide inside, glance back at Sylvain's apartment as though seeing it for the first time, then drive off as quickly as possible, as though fleeing the arms of a depraved mistress, you cross over the north bridge, take the highway, back to your town, its quiet streets, but you drive fast, extremely fast, and there's the cement wall on the curve getting closer and closer, but you don't slow down, but you don't turn, your expression hardens, you clutch the steering wheel, then suddenly you stomp on the brakes, a shrieking, yours and that of the tires, the car stops a few centimetres from the wall, but not you, you keep on shrieking and shrieking, and when the car pulls up in front of your house a few minutes later and you get out, the interior is still ringing with the echo of your cries, but the same people wait outside, their feet in the snow, four of them, cameras still, mics still, you avoid their gaze, no comment, don't insist, nothing to say, still calm but your voice more impatient than this morning, yet they don't give up, they insist, they follow you right to your door and just before you step inside, you see two neighbours down the street, watching the scene, curious, voyeurs, and finally you close the door, finally you drop into an armchair, finally you stop moving, the television still on, the screen blue, your gaze pans over the room, stops on each object for long minutes, a family picture on the wall, a landscape on the other wall, sports DVDs in the bookcase, the fireplace, two plants on each corner, the coffee table holding the knick-knacks Judith collected, Alexis' toys strewn in a corner, the more you burn your eyes on the relics, the more your eyeballs sink back into their sockets, as though about to fall deep inside you, the phone rings several times during the course of the lengthy examination but you don't answer, then hunger, seven o'clock, it's dark outside, you walk to the kitchen, heat up yesterday's leftover tourtière, eat it with ketchup, study the kitchen with the same intensity as you did the living room, mesmerized by each object, by the order, by the clean counters, then you start digging through the pantry, pull out the bread, the peanut butter, the cheese, you make two sandwiches and wash them down with some grape juice, the children's grape juice, you're no longer hungry but you swallow anyway, stuff your face, cram food inside, ice cream, cookies, cake, you burp, grimace in pain, clutch your belly with both hands but you don't stop and you put nothing away and you don't close the jars and you leave crumbs everywhere, then you feel nauseous, you raise your hand to your mouth but you don't budge, you don't walk to the bathroom, you open your mouth instead and it gushes, it spurts, it spatters onto the island, a long stream of vomit splashing everywhere, you wipe your mouth and return to the living room where you stay until late, inert, then you stand up, take the stairs to your room, remove your clothes and lie down after slipping on the nasal mask, the sleep apnea machine you've hooked yourself up to for the past two years, the one that was so hard to get used to but was purported to be so essential, the doctor said so

– You're thirty-three, you're still young, but in a few years' time you'll be at a greater risk for a heart attack and sleep apnea increases that risk. My advice is that you get the machine. It's a bother, but it's good for you. It increases the odds of your having a better quality of life.

two

years ago, you close your eyes, the mask on your face sends a continuous flow of air but you don't fall asleep, you even start to shake, you get up and go to the children's room, you look at the twin beds, especially Alexis' still with its safety rails, suddenly you rip them off, smash them against the wall, bash the toys, the pictures, the beds, everything shatters, splinters, shards pierce your arms and cheek, then you collapse in tears surrounded by the devastation you've wreaked, finally sleep, dreamless, until late the next morning, the front doorbell awakens you, you lie there as it rings three, four, five times, finally silence, you get up, go to the window, a car pulls away, Alexandre, a friend who lives nearby, you walk through the wreckage to the bathroom, examine the minuscule cut on your cheek, grab the bottle of antiseptic, open it, but you stop halfway, but you study the bottle, but you hesitate, your reflection in the mirror, then you bring the bottle

19

to your lips, you take a mouthful of antiseptic, hold it there without swallowing, staring at your reflection, then you spit at the mirror, your reflection dripping now, as though you were melting, and you sit down on the toilet bowl, and you defecate, and you stand up, study your excrement, finally you leave, go down to the kitchen, the sight of the mess and the vomit makes you wrinkle your nose, you listen to the messages on the answering machine, Judith's family one after another, shattered, in shock, especially her mother, hysterical, and the two messages from reporters wanting an interview and a message from Jean-Marc who has looked after everything, who wants to explain it all to you, who expects to hear back from you soon, and you listen carefully to this last message, then you rewind the tape to listen to it again and again, and each time your features harden a bit more, especially on hearing certain words, "details," "look after," "signatures," and finally you slam down the receiver, your lips clenched so tight they hurt, you collect yourself and call Jean-Marc, he asks how you are then stops short, awkward, I'm sure he regrets his stupid question but it's too late, in fact you ask him if he actually wants an answer to his "fucking moronic question," he stammers an apology, you add that you too are sorry, but your voice is just as cold, then he explains that there are all kinds of things to be signed, he offers to come to you, but you would rather meet him at his office, he says he isn't working today, he's incapable of it, as though stating the obvious, almost a reproach, but you insist, you don't want to go to his house, you don't want him to come here, so grudgingly he agrees to meet you in his office, you hang up, time to make breakfast, but the kitchen is a shambles with traces of vomit, dirt and filth, so you escape to the living room with your plate, eat seated on the couch, stay put for a good hour, leave the plate and cup on the floor and go upstairs to your bedroom, a glance through your closet, but you end up wearing the same clothes as yesterday except for the underwear, main floor, coat, boots, old worn boots Judith hated to see, always pestering you to choose new ones, you've got a sports store after all, there's nothing simpler than finding a new pair, she made fun of you and your boots, you leave the house, recognize the two reporters kicking their heels on the sidewalk, they race over, like hounds having caught their quarry's scent, but before they have time to speak you

– Sonofabitch, I kept calm, told you no, all for what! Be civilized, do the right thing, none of it matters. Shit! Nothing matters!

explode, bend over, grab a handful of snow, make a sloppy snowball, and you throw it and you yell, and you throw other snowballs at them, they bolt, back to their cars, and speed away, and you keep throwing projectiles at the cars by now out of range, then you stop, a ready-made snowball in your right hand, look around, see your neighbour Michel there, using his lunch hour to make a snowfort for his children, his three children playmates of Béatrice's, he's there, outside, his shovel partly buried in the snow, paralyzed, dismayed, you hold his gaze, as though challenging him, finally he stammers a few words, he saw *it* in the newspapers, he mumbles words like "dreadful," "horrible," your expression softens, an inaudible "thanks" escapes your dry lips, you take it all in, the half-built snowfort, Michel's house, his three children's sleds, you slowly pulverize the snowball in your hand, then you walk, no, you run away to your car, Michel's voice behind you *"if you need anything…",* you slam the door on the absurdity of his words, take off, feeling as though you're about to vomit all over again, but the feeling passes, highway, north bridge, the City, downtown, your brother-in-law's large architect's office, you sit facing him, he has bags under his eyes, he's in a sorry state, he tells you the viewing at the funeral home is scheduled for Thursday and the service for Friday morning, many more details about money, inheritance, technicalities that barely register with you, too busy contemplating the high-tech design, the modern art on the walls, the window with its view of the City, and when Jean-Marc holds out several documents for you to sign, you look up, your eyes uncomprehending, but your voice calm, almost

- But I did the same as you. Not the same job, that's true: you studied and all that, me I've got no education, but I worked hard, I opened my store, I succeeded. I did what I had to do, just as much as you …

clinical, he gulps, straightens one of the few strands of hair on his balding pate, blinks in discomfort, and the words he utters in a

22

– I guess that . . . that's no guarantee . . .

quavering voice make your eyebrows shoot up, your jaw drop, as though you're struck by a revelation, and I think that is when you understood, even though there's really nothing to understand, nothing at all, and you don't move, don't speak and Jean-Marc has to hold the documents out again before you react, bend over, sign them unread, then he gives you the funeral home address, it's not far from where you live, finally you leave, you head out, you take off, your cell phone rings several times but you don't answer, you're back at the house by three, you step out of your car, then notice the red van in front of Michel's house, a van that doesn't belong to your neighbour or to his wife Lucie who doesn't work and is a stay-at-home mom, you walk up to your front door, a piece of paper taped there, a message from a neighbour Rick explaining he dropped by to see how you were doing, that he's heard the news, saying you can call him anytime, you crumple the paper, step inside, sit in the living room, study what's left of your breakfast, long minutes pass, movement in the street glimpsed through the window, you take a closer look, a guy seems to be leaving Michel's house, a man in his thirties who walks to the red van, looks around suspiciously, gets into the van and starts the engine, you turn to look at your neighbour's house, a quiet house, a normal house, you walk to the bathroom, stop, return to the living room and urinate in a corner, you sit back down and you do nothing, a quivering in your eye, a stirring inside your head, the slow shifting of quicksand, then people walk by, children return home from school, you don't get up to look out the window, you lie down on the couch, you curl into a ball, you close your eyes, you hide them with your fists and you weep, you weep in a silence that buries all living sound, seventy-five minutes, you get up, put on your coat and boots, make your way to the closest restaurant, a thirty-minute walk or so, but once there, you don't dare go inside, and I think I know why, you used to come here with Judith and the children, once a fortnight, you keep on going, you stop at the next restaurant, a chic Italian eatery you've only been to once or twice before, you step into an elegant dining room, more than a dozen customers including a married couple, vague acquaintances in fact, both wave with a smile, clearly still in the dark, you stare at them, expressionless, not responding to their greeting, they frown at your stony silence, mutter to each other then ignore you, you eat exceedingly slowly, then do nothing, not even once you've finished, not even when the bill is brought to you, total inertia, the waitress returns to ask if you're all right, you say yes and don't move, twenty minutes, vaguely you notice the curious glances the couple sends your way, the waitress returns, polite, makes it clear you must go, other customers are waiting, you can plainly see the many empty tables but you don't insist, you get up, you pay and you step outside, it's dark and cold out, you don't do up your coat, you take the longest route home, impossible detours, ninety minutes instead of forty, you're frozen to the bone when you finally step inside, lock the door, roam through the house, stop to stare at your twenty-six sports DVDs purchased over the past three years, then you give up on choosing one, just turn on the big 50-inch TV that you bought yourself two months ago, lie down on the couch and, remote in hand, you listen to the news, the economic crisis, a look back at Haiti's earthquake, the rape and murder of a young woman, the main suspect an escaped prisoner from Donnacona who's been on the loose for a number of years, but when your story comes up, you change the channel, then switch from one channel to the next, never stopping for more than thirty seconds on any given show, then around midnight you come across a channel showing nothing, all done, all dark, you drop the remote, cross your hands between your cheek and the armrest of the couch and stare at the black screen, you fall into the screen, you close your eyes and dream of that darkness, that emptiness, and the nothingness turns out to be the worst possible nightmare, and when you awaken around ten, your face is wet with tears, you sit up, you're cold, but you don't turn up the heat, you light a fire in the hearth, twigs, newspaper, logs, flames shoot up, but you decide not to close the fire screen, you back up to the middle of the room, you watch the flames, then a spark shoots out from the fireplace, lands on the old newspapers scattered across the floor, the paper starts to smoulder, but you don't respond, you don't intervene, you watch, the small flame simply scorches the paper before dying out, you sigh then and leave the living room, finally you listen to all your messages, those at home and on your cell phone, friends, store employees, your brother crying asking where you are, whether or not you've told Dad and Mom in Florida, he begs you to call him, they all want you to call, they all exclaim how horrible it is, they all offer their help, but you make just one phone call, to your store, you speak to your manager, advise him you won't be back for quite a while, he asks for instructions, but you tell him to do whatever he wants, he says he'd like to have some specifics and even though you can tell how unnerved he is, you say again that he can do whatever he wants, that it doesn't matter at all, not in the least, not at all, and you hang up, the doorbell rings, you can make out two silhouettes behind the glass, you panic, hurry down to the basement, the doorbell rings again, you can even hear the sound of the doorknob being turned several times in vain, finally silence, you look around you, children's decorations, shelves full of toys, posters of cartoon heroes, dolls, trucks and figurines, and in a corner your elliptical trainer that you've not touched in three days, you who normally trains every morning before work, you get on the elliptical and start to pedal, a firm grip on the handles propelling your arms back and forth, and you pedal, and you row, you jack up the resistance as far as it will go, and you pedal, and you row, and you go as fast as possible, you grimace, you perspire profusely, you clench your teeth, your limbs begin to tremble from the strain but you don't slow down, you keep on pushing and pushing, ten minutes, then fifteen, then twenty, thirty, forty-five minutes pushing yourself to the limit, without respite, your body sticky with sweat under your sopping clothes, your face crimson, your breath wheezing, you slow down against your will, you grunt, you cry out, you don't want to stop, but suddenly you flatten your hand over your heart and groan in pain, you collapse to the floor, on your back, convulsing, gasping for air, clenching and unclenching your fingers on your burning chest, but the pain lessens, your heart starts beating normally, the heart attack didn't want you after all, your breathing stabilizes and you close your eyes, you lie there, thirty minutes, silence, silence, you get up, your legs rubbery, take the stairs, bathroom, a long hot shower, then you throw on the first clothes you come across, you return to the main floor, two o'clock, you step outside, without a coat, your slippers on, it's cold out but the sun is shining, you walk to the sidewalk and look at the houses on the street, orderly, pretty, well-kept, peaceful, and the red van is back in front of Michel's house, you narrow your eyes, then you return inside, look up a phone number, dial, give your neighbour's name to the insurance company receptionist, then Michel answers, surprised and a bit awkward at your call, so you tell him there's no point to it all, but he doesn't understand, you continue, your voice

– *Your house, your kids, your family, your job . . . It's all for nothing, Michel.*

a monotone, he says again that he doesn't understand, fumbles as he asks you what he can do to help, you tell him he'd better come home right away, immediately, then he'll understand, you hang up, examine the mess in the kitchen, go outside, still coatless, walk over to the sidewalk, your hands in your pockets, and you wait, ten minutes, fifteen, then Michel's car drives past, Michel steps out of the vehicle, Michel stares at you in concern and suspicion, Michel asks what's going on, and you turn your head toward the red van, your neighbour sees it now too, a flicker of doubt in his eye, he quicksteps to the house, ninety seconds, shouts and exclamations burst from within the pretty bungalow, so you return inside, stop in the living room, look at the fire in the hearth, several sparks have singed the wooden floor, but that's all, you sit down on the couch, see the red van speed past the window, the phone rings, this time you do answer, it's your brother Alain, whom you've barely seen since he moved to Drummondville, Alain shouting, chewing you out, asking you why you didn't call back, and you simply say you didn't want to, he bursts into tears then, he apologizes, he asks if you've told Dad and Mom in Florida, you say no, then he announces he's coming to stay with you right away, you say that's out of the question, you'll see him at the funeral home tomorrow, you give him the address and the time, finally he backs down but insists that tomorrow he'll stay with you until the service on Friday and even all weekend, he, Marie-Hélène and the children, they'll be there for you, they won't abandon you, you say fine, provided they all make it there tomorrow, he's surprised, says of course they'll be there, without fail, but you insist, without a trace of irony or

- That's if your house doesn't burn down tonight. Or if a burglar doesn't rob you overnight. Or if your children come home from school this afternoon. Maybe they'll be attacked on their way home. Maybe some maniac will kidnap them, torture them for hours then kill them.

malice, and the silence stretches on and on, interrupted only by Alain's breathing, but finally he speaks, his voice disconcerted, a tad resentful, he understands how despair might make you say things *"that make no sense,"* but his last words make you scream, spit, splutter into

- Why wouldn't it make any sense? Tell me that! He gives fuck all whether something makes sense or not! He doesn't give a flying fuck!

the phone, and a frantic Alain asks who it is you're talking about, but you don't reply, you might not even know yourself, at least not clearly, and you throw the phone at the wall, and you go back to the living room, and you glare defiantly at the fireplace, but the fire is almost out, so you add more logs cursing unintelligibly, you stir the embers, and the fire springs back to life, flaming, triumphant, once more you don't close the fire screen, coat, boots, then out you go, leaving the front door wide open, and as you back your car into the street, you see Michel, furious, emerging from his house, he strides to his car with Lucie on his heels, Lucie in her dressing gown, Lucie in a panic, Lucie in tears, begging and imploring, but you're not interested, you drive away, you pass your friend Alexandre coming in the opposite direction, no doubt on his way to your house, and Alexandre must have recognized your car too because in your rearview mirror you see him pull a U-turn, probably in the hope of catching up with you, but you get a good head start, you lose him, and make your way then to the closest hotel, you book a room, you watch TV, you don't answer your cell phone when it rings a half-dozen times, and you fall asleep, extremely late, an anguished and turbulent sleep, peopled with screams and fury, and you wake up at ten, eat in the hotel restaurant and return home, the front door still wide open, you walk inside, astonished to see everything still in order, nothing has been stolen or vandalized, and the fire in the hearth is out, and nothing has burned within, so you go back outside and your cries tumble down the

- But this was the time! Why not now? Hey? Why not now?

street, deserted but for a woman farther down staring at you, you give her the finger, you go back inside and close the door behind you, and you cry, wander, and you cry, for two hours, and you end up upstairs in your bedroom, black pants, black suit jacket, white shirt and black tie, you study yourself for a moment in the mirror, indifferent, then go out, closing the door behind you this time and locking it, and just before you start up the car you stare at the house for a long time, a long, long time, as though your eyes already knew something your conscious mind had yet to grasp, then you drive, ten minutes, the funeral home, already four or five visitors seemingly embarrassed to see you show up a half-hour late, the three caskets, closed, you go from one to the next, your jaw clenched, thin-lipped, then the handshakes, the condolences, the sobs, the curses against fate, Judith's mother who's in such deep despair she has to be held up, and you say almost nothing, then Jean-Marc and his family, Jean-Marc who whispers in your ear that everything is under control but you need to meet with the funeral director before the afternoon is out to sign some papers and settle up, then your brother Alain and his family, his wife who can't stop crying, her tears on your neck, Alain who says he's told Dad and Mom, who's surprised they didn't call, but you tell him you haven't picked up your messages since yesterday, and Alain shakes his head, says that Dad and Mom will be on the first plane, assures you they will no doubt be back by tomorrow or even tonight, then still other people who gradually appear, including a shattered Alexandre, who swears he drove to your place on several occasions, and you remain silent, withdrawn, your cousin Juliette approaches, thin, her face already all wrinkled at the age of forty-eight, her wheelchair propelled by her husband Normand, her eyes full of compassion, and what she says to you

- I know it's hard to accept, but everything happens for a reason . . .

lights a furtive but intense blaze in your pupils, you open your mouth to reply but a friend of Judith's steps up to hug you, then other people, more and more, finally you ask Jean-Marc how it is that so many people know when you told no one, but Jean-Marc thought of everything, Jean-Marc placed a notice in two daily newspapers, Jean-Marc started a couple of telephone trees, you nod, look around you, all the people, all the faces, some just a blur, some you don't recognize, then you spot cousin Juliette again, over there, and you head in her direction, eyes hardening, but she speaks first before you get a chance to, says she wants to go out for a cigarette but Normand has gone to the bathroom, would you be good enough to take her outside if it's no bother, you help her on with her coat, you slip on your own coat, you push her wheelchair, people step back respectfully, outside the cold is mild, the sun bright, you head for the disabled ramp and start to wheel her down slowly, making an effort to ease the chair down the incline, then you lean over so your cousin can hear you, you say that, if you've understood correctly, the accident that crippled her at the age of twenty-seven happened for a reason, and she nods, swears she's stronger now, you nod, the weight of the wheelchair too much to hold back, and suddenly you don't anymore, the chair heads down the ramp on its own now, picking up speed, your cousin asking what's going on, and you do nothing, the wheelchair heads straight for the street with Juliette yelping, Juliette fumbling in vain at the wheels with her feeble hands, Juliette coming to a standstill at last right in the middle of the street just as a car slams on its brakes, and a second car rear-ends the first, and at last you walk over to Juliette, you lean in from behind, and your voice

– What about now, do you feel strong now?

is low, so low, and you notice that Juliette is gasping, Juliette's eyes are wide, Juliette is about to pass out, and at last you look around you, the woman driver in the first car transfixed with fear behind the steering wheel, the driver of the second car stepping out of his vehicle, a hand up to his bloody nose, your friends and family streaming out of the funeral home, including Normand who races to his wife's side, panic-stricken, yelling for someone to call an ambulance, Juliette's having a heart attack, and everyone rushes about, asking questions, turning in circles, and you watch the chaos in fascination, motionless, a steadfast rock in a storm-swept sea, but someone grabs you by your arm, your brother Alain, eyes rolling, asks what happened, but you disengage yourself gently, take a few steps back as though to better grasp the whole debacle, as though to burn it with a branding iron on your mind, as though to photograph it in pixels of fire, then you turn on your heel and walk away, ignoring your brother's calls, and you climb into your car, and you take off, you call

Sylvain from your cell phone but there's no answer, you don't leave a message, your fuel gauge shows next to empty, stop at a gas station, fill up, you go inside to pay and on your way out, you notice the bank machine in a corner of the gas station, you walk over and withdraw the maximum the machine will allow, a thousand dollars, and you're off again, you drive toward the City, you cross the north bridge, fifteen minutes, you park, you enter the bar Le Maquis, the server greets you warmly, she remembers you even though you only come once every five or six weeks, you ask if she's seen Sylvain, yes, last night, he seemed quite down, she says you don't look too good yourself, you order a beer and sit down at an empty table, happy hour has started, lots of customers, men and women in their thirties, talking, laughing, arguing, drinking, good humour, your cell phone rings often, each time you check the caller, each time you see it's not Sylvain, each time you don't bother answering, but after an hour, you can't stand the ringing anymore so you turn it off, another beer, happy hour's over, fewer customers, the clock shows eight, you leave to pee, you return, another beer, your fourth, your eyes on the door, then for the first time you study the people around you, a young woman on her own over there, in her thirties, pretty, long chestnut-brown hair, she looks at you insistently and even smiles finally, you look away immediately, as you've done whenever a young woman starts to flirt with you, and I know you've developed the reflex to avoid temptation and trouble and disorder, yes, to avoid all that, and suddenly Sylvain appears in a black shirt and dark jacket, he sees you, is reassured, walks over to sit across from you, he's come from the funeral home, everyone's looking for you, your brother and your brother-in-law have been trying to reach you on your cell phone, Sylvain himself tried to call you three times, so why didn't you answer, why did you leave the funeral parlour, why are you here, and your silence starts to annoy Sylvain, finally you say that you want to get loaded, Sylvain calms down then, orders two beers, he tells you he understands your confusion, tells you that and much more about the absurdity of life and suffering and injustice, but you're not really listening, you watch the waitress as she brings both your drinks, her suggestive grin in your friend's direction, her firm buttocks in her figure-hugging short skirt, and you interrupt Sylvain to ask if he's ever fucked the waitress, he's taken aback, but he does answer yes, and, with no hint of a smile, you ask him if she likes it hot and dirty, and he, still more disconcerted, says yes, quite a bit, you nod, staring into space now, slowly you start to speak, your voice distant, you explain that Judith didn't like it hot and dirty, at least hadn't for several years, you still made love once a week, sometimes twice, but it was much tamer, especially since the children's arrival, and she was often tired, or in a hurry, or both, so sex never lasted very long, not to mention you always had to check first, no spontaneity, nothing impromptu, but from what your other couple friends have said, you told yourself that all things considered, the two of you were within the norm, yes, the norm, you repeat it several times, the norm, and Sylvain doesn't interrupt you, stares at you in silence, alarmed, then you sigh, look around and declare that you would like to do it hot and dirty with someone tonight, and you say the words with an odd lassitude, and Sylvain points out this is definitely not a good time, you get worked up a bit then, you

- Why not? It hasn't been a good time for nine whole years! I've been keeping a lid on it for nine whole years, always doing the right thing, and what good was that, eh? What good was that?

attract
stares, Sylvain begs you to calm down, which you do eventually, but you throw back your beer, and your friend tries to reason with you, states you need to go back to the funeral home, everyone's waiting, someone told him one of your cousins almost had a heart attack earlier on but that she's out of danger now, you tell him you know all that, you were the cause, Sylvain doesn't understand, you explain, he stares at you then, outraged, how could you push her wheelchair into the street, you point out you didn't push her, but hearing her bullshit, you simply lost any desire to keep holding onto the wheelchair, you wanted her gone from you, actually you're not really sure what you wanted, to let go, just let go, but you couldn't have predicted she would roll right onto the street, or that a car would nearly hit her, or that a second car would run into the first, or that your cousin would come that close to having a heart attack, no, you couldn't have predicted

that the mere loosening of your fingers would provoke such a chain reaction, just as Judith and your children couldn't have predicted that they would die on their drive home, no one can predict anything, no one can know anything, no matter how well-organized, how well-prepared, how much in control, or more specifically how much a person feels in control, and you get excited again, you ask your friend if he remembers when you were teenagers, how irresponsible and disruptive you were, how you didn't give a damn about a thing, how when you came home from parties totally hammered you'd still drive your parents' cars, or how you skated on the lake during the early April thaw, and then you got older, you came round, like everyone does, or at least, you came round even if he didn't, and the whole while you thump on the table as though trying to squash the phrase, pulverize it, and you raise your

– Me, the sucker, I swallowed it all: take responsibility, prepare for the future, get your life in order. . . But you got it! You got that it's all pointless, you didn't change and you were right!

voice, but Sylvain retorts it isn't that simple, so you bang even harder on the table, you yell at him to stop lying, everyone has been lying to you for years but not him, he's not allowed, not your best friend, and you get to your feet, intent on leaving, on hitting every single bar, you want to get pissed with Sylvain like you used to, hey, Sylvain, c'mon, let's go, but Sylvain looks somber, Sylvain doesn't want to go,

Sylvain tries to pacify you, you don't understand, you remind him he's usually the first to jump at the prospect of a party, he loses patience then, gets to his feet, says you're upset, urges you to go back to the funeral home where everyone's waiting, but you yell you don't want to go back, you yell you want to stay here, you yell as loud as you can, Sylvain grabs your shoulder then, says okay, fine, don't go back there, but he begs you to come to his place instead, right now, you'll keep talking and drinking all night long in his apartment, but that's not what you want, you want to get out, erupt like a volcano that's lain dormant for too long, and you've started back on your litany of excess when Dan, the owner, comes over to ask you to leave the premises, because by now everyone is looking at you, annoyed and apprehensive, but Sylvain knows Dan well, takes him by the arm, leads him aside for a talk, you sit, wait, glare at the other patrons, and once more you notice the pretty girl on her own, who's still watching you, but this time you don't look away, this time you raise your glass in her direction, this time you wave her over, and she, after a moment's hesitation, stands up, walks toward you, sits down on the chair you motion to with your chin, and you tell her that just three days ago, you would never have dared invite a beautiful girl over to have a drink with you, that you would have been too afraid of any problems that could cause, and you give a joyless laugh while the girl nods, then you ask her her name, Mélanie, so you ask Mélanie if she would like to go out with you tonight, another moment's indecision, then she agrees, her voice calm, which is when Sylvain comes back to tell you he's smoothed things over with Dan, but you get up, announce you're going out with Mélanie, invite your friend to come along, but Sylvain refuses, discouraged, Sylvain begs you to be reasonable, and you get angry all over again, you yell at him, how can he ask you that, him, your friend, but you see a furious Dan approaching so you throw on your coat, grab Mélanie, who has her coat on by now too, by the hand, head for the door, and Mélanie hesitates slightly but finally does follow you, she says her car isn't far, but you insist on taking yours parked out front, you open the car door and see Sylvain coming out of the bar, looking for you, but you order him not to follow you, you don't want to see him again, he stops but begs you not to do anything stupid, call him later, crash at his place, but you get in the car, Mélanie too, the doors slam, the car takes off, Mélanie is worried, haven't you had too much to drink to be driving, but no, you only had four or five beer, she asks where you want to go, you have no idea, other than Le Maquis you don't know many bars in Montréal, actually the ones you hung out at over ten years ago must attract a crowd much younger than you by now, so she suggests a little bar she knows, right next to her place, that way you won't have to drive if you have too much to drink, all spoken as naturally as can be, you shoot her a knowing glance, but she looks straight ahead as she gives you directions, the neighbourhood you're now in is on the poorer side of town that you don't know all that well, finally you park, you both get out of the car, you follow Mélanie into a bar, Le Losange, a fairly shabby interior, slot machines at the back, so-so music, a dozen seedy-looking customers, for the first time you notice that Mélanie's clothes are a little worse-for-wear themselves, not that that lessens her desirability, you find a table, the server comes over, her outfit too sexy for her body, she greets Mélanie like an old acquaintance, Mélanie introduces you, her name is Guylaine, Guylaine sizes you up quite openly, amused by your suit jacket and tie, you order two shooters, Mélanie refuses at first but you insist so she accepts, downs her drink in one go without pulling a face, then you order two beer, Mélanie still hasn't said anything, just looks at you often, you ask her why she agreed to come with you tonight, and her answer

   – *Because you're suffering.*

                    rattles you somewhat, you ask if it shows that much, she doesn't answer but her silence speaks volumes, you drain your beer and laugh condescendingly, she doesn't react, you look deep into her eyes, her gentle but sad eyes, and point out she doesn't look like she's in such great shape herself, she half-smiles, her voice barely more than a

   – *You see, it's not that hard to tell . . .*

                    breath of air and yet you hear her over the background music, but you shake your head, as though you don't like the direction your conversation has taken, and you order two more shooters, Guylaine brings two glasses but Mélanie doesn't want to drink anymore, you insist but in vain, so you drink them both, you speak then, yes, you're suffering, you admit it, but you don't feel like talking about it, just like you don't want to know why Mélanie isn't doing all that well herself, just like you don't give a crap about anyone else's suffering, because tonight is a night for living it up, because dammit! we're all going to die so we might as well make the most of it, and your companion listens in silence, her expression sad, and you're fed up with her gloominess, so you suggest going back to her place, she agrees immediately, Guylaine waves coyly as you leave, there's a cold wind blowing, you make as though to take your car but Mélanie says you've had too much to drink, anyway she lives just one block over, so you start to walk, you say a little stroll in the crisp night air will only make you appreciate the warmth of her body all the more, and you snicker, surprised at your own audacity, yet I remember when you were single, how you were always quite brazen with the ladies, but Mélanie looks serious all of a sudden and tells you there'll be no sex, which throws you for quite a loop, you try a bit of provocation, tell her girls who take guys home rarely want to play Parcheesi, at least not in your day they didn't, but she shakes

– *No, not tonight. That's not what you need. Me either.*

her head, you pout, you mutter oh no, this can't be happening, you tell her to stop jerking your chain, but she doesn't back down, so you turn on your heel, walk to your car, she cries after you that you shouldn't be driving but you ignore her, she calls out for you to wait a second, you turn thinking she's changed her mind but when you see her digging through her purse and scribbling something on a scrap of paper, you begin walking again, get into your car, start to close the door but Mélanie is there, holding out a piece of paper, it's her address, she's usually at home in the evenings, you can drop by whenever you want, you take the paper scornfully, stuff it in your coat pocket and start up the car without a word, a quick check in the rearview mirror, she's still standing in the street, all alone, turned to watch your car as it drives off, you scowl, frustrated, the clock on the dashboard reads eleven fifteen, you drive aimlessly, straight in front of you, a traffic light about a hundred metres away, it turns red, but you don't slow down, but you keep going, but you drive right through the intersection and feel little surprise when the other car hits you on the passenger side, it shakes you up a bit but not too much, you take your time getting out, the other driver, in his fifties, approaches, furious, he wants to know why you didn't slow down, why you didn't stop for the red light, his questions tumble over each other, punctuated with many a flourish, you listen calmly, wearing an ambiguous grin, as though biding your time, and when he finally stops to catch his breath, it's your turn, your words slurred because

- Didn't expect that, did ya? Thought you'd be home in ten minutes in your warm bed like usual! No reason for it to be any different, right? But I was here, that's all it took. I came out of nowhere. That's the way it is, my man! That's the way it is!

of the alcohol, he stares at you then, bewildered, finally he seems to clue into the fact that you've been drinking, you reach for your cell phone, he asks what you're doing, you tell him you're calling the police, you tell him not to worry, you'll tell them it was your fault, no problem, but he's not the least bit reassured, in fact he starts getting genuinely alarmed, he stammers there must be a way to settle this without involving the police, c'mon, why complicate matters, and he hands you his business card, and he invites you to call him tomorrow, you open your eyes wide, surprised, then you understand, you give a knowing look, he doesn't want his wife to know he was in the City tonight, that's it, or he has drugs in his car, or something along those lines, isn't that right, and he finds the allusions even more distressing, he shoots a hunted look at the couple of curious bystanders watching off to one side, then he steps up to you, reiterates that the cops mustn't come, promises he'll pay you tomorrow, you study his fear then, yes, his fear, next you slide his card into your pocket, tell him he can go, and the guy sighs, he thanks you, he shakes your hand, but you raise a finger, add that you won't call the police tonight, of course, but tomorrow, you just might, who's to know, or the day after tomorrow, or another day, who knows, or never, actually you have no idea, you'll have to see, it will depend on your mood, in any case, you have his card should you need it, and all colour drains from the guy's face as he listens, you put a hand on his shoulder, your voice is unctuous but

– From now on, it's me who's got the power to screw up your life . . . or not . . . You'll have to go about life knowing you don't call the shots . . . That's what lucidity is. You're a lucky man.

final, and he's on the verge of tears, he insists, he'll give you loads of money if you'll just call him tomorrow, he swears, but no cops, no, not the police, you're already getting into your car, you drive off, without looking back, but after eight or nine blocks, the engine hiccoughs, sputters, the fuel gauge on empty, but you just filled it up not long ago, you park at a fast food joint that's open twenty-four hours, you get out, peer under the car, see gas dripping to the ground, must be a crack caused by the collision, so you abandon your vehicle and start to walk, your hands in your pockets, you pull out the guy's business card, look at it for a minute, then tear it into small pieces that you drop behind you, the breeze is light but freezing, you turn up your coat collar, you reach a busier boulevard, pedestrians, cars, a nightclub disgorging dozens of patrons, must be the end of a show, you stop, you watch them laughing and talking among themselves, you sigh, then you pull out your cell phone, snap it open and punch in the first digits for Sylvain's number but you stop, upset, and eventually put your cell phone back in your coat but it starts ringing almost immediately, you check to see who's calling, your brother, you rub your forehead, turn back to the dozens of people milling about across the street from the club, your expression sinister, and suddenly you hurl your phone in their direction, but up high, as high as you can, you watch it rise, become lost for a second or two in the darkness, then hurtle back down, toward the crowd, but it hits no one, it plunges into the snow a few centimetres from the feet of a young woman who remains totally oblivious, your lips pull back into a bitter, ironic smirk, you cross the street, approach the woman and

   – You've got no clue what a close call you just had . . .

                                     she, clearly tipsy, has no idea what you're talking about and giggles, you keep on walking then, now you're in a posher neighbourhood, lots of hustle and bustle, you stare at the people whose path you cross, they ignore you, you pick a bar at random, enter, the place is more stylish and trendier than Le Losange, there's even a no-nonsense bouncer, not too many people, mostly couples or small groups, two girls, both pretty and sexy, alone at the bar, you walk over, offer them a drink, the brush-off, annoyance, heads turned, you don't insist, you down a shooter, then another, make your way to the bathroom, empty your bladder, totter slightly on your return, you're drunk and it shows, you repeat your offer and one of the two girls, fed up, tells you to leave them alone, you lose it then, you yell at them then, you unload on them then, if they don't want to be hit on, why go to bars alone wearing sexy clothes, they should just stay home, dammit, and they stare at you, dumbfounded, call you a bastard, a frustrated bastard, and you shoot back that they're right there, damn right, you're frustrated, have been for years, just like everyone else, just like them, you're sure they are, everyone is frustrated over something or other, you insist, so why not get rid of the frustration together, eh, right now, a threesome, a first for you, at thirty-five it's about time, isn't it, and what about you girls, have you already been in one, but you don't give them time to answer, you're in a hurry, you order them to follow you, now, c'mon, let's go, quick, you even take each of them by the arm, they yell at you, try to get away, but another pair of hands swoops down on your shoulders, it's the bouncer, direction exit, you protest, not much, for form's sake, and you find yourself out on the sidewalk, and you lean against a wall, and you close your eyes, you look as though you might throw up but the moment passes, you start to stagger down the street, weaving, take a few seconds to get your bearings, keep walking and walking, eventually find and slide into your car, and you stare at the frozen expanse before you, and tears roll down your cheeks, and you're asleep before the tears have had time to freeze, it's the cold that wakes you, you're frozen stiff, the clock on the dash reads six, you take off your tie and throw it onto the back seat, you get out, your head's pounding but it's bearable, you shiver on your way into the first open café, a coffee, a muffin, you slowly drink and eat sitting at a table, stare at the three other customers, they look lonely, they look depressed, and you don't budge from the table, two hours, you close your eyes and fall asleep, the waitress wakes you, tells you you can't sleep here, the clock on the wall reads nine thirty, you leave, a light snowfall, you stare at the ground, your boots beneath you, the soles of your boots splashing, slush on the sidewalk, the metro station, you head inside, pay for a ticket, stand studying the map for a long time, maybe you're remembering just how much Alexis loved coming to Montréal to take the metro, just like you when you were a kid, I even remember that you used to dream of driving the metro, yes, all that may be crossing your mind, finally you choose a direction, the platform is almost deserted, rush hour is over, the train stops in front of you, you step inside, remain standing, holding onto the centre pole with your right hand, the train rocks its way through the tunnel, a couple sits across from you, a baby stroller in front of them, an old woman sits farther up, the young couple murmurs sweet nothings, the young couple smiles, the young couple kisses, the young couple is alone in the world, as for you, you eye them witheringly, and you turn to look at the stroller, and you see the sleeping baby, and you turn back to the couple, to their smiles, to their cooing, to their kissing, then the train stops, the doors open, no one stands to leave, the couple still lost in loverland, the couple oblivious to one and all, you give the stroller a push then, quick but firm, and the stroller rolls outside a second before the doors close, the couple must realize then something's amiss nearby because at last they stop devouring each other with their eyes, turn to look, jump to their feet, glance frantically left and right, finally the woman sees the stroller on the platform and starts to scream, slowly the train starts up again, the man's hands tear at the doors, the train already in the tunnel, the woman's screams, and her tears, and her cries for help, suddenly the man wheels on you to ask what happened, you say nothing, you gaze calmly at the two of them, he asks a second time, shouting, panic-stricken, hysterical, in stark contrast with your calm, your silence, your fascination, he grabs you then by the collar, shakes you, asks if you're the one who did this, his eyes rolling in rage and incomprehension, and his spouse grabs for the emergency lever on the wall, practically pulls it off, twice, three times, but nothing happens, no bell rings, the woman shrieks that it's broken, you can't help a strident laugh then, devoid of gaiety, the harshest sound to have ever crossed your lips, and your voice is as empty as

– *What were the chances of that alarm not working? One in a thousand? In ten thousand?*

your life, the guy punches you then, a right hook to your left cheek, and he bellows asking whether you're crazy, whether you're the one who pushed the stroller, you fall to the floor, he kicks you twice, you take the beating, you make no move to defend yourself, you don't budge, you feel the metro stopping, you hear the woman scream at her spouse to hurry, they've got to catch the train going the other way, running footsteps, cries and sobs growing distant, the train starts up again, slowly you get to your feet, just in time to see the couple make a dash for the platform stairs before the train vanishes into the tunnel, you sit, rub your bright red cheek, your aching belly, the old woman farther up eyes you in horror, you ignore her and stare into the emptiness, then you get off at the next station, take the stairs to street level, the heart of downtown, a light snow falls still, you walk aimlessly, cross streets without looking, are honked at several times but you don't react, you peer at each business you pass, restaurants, clothing stores, movie theatres, jewellery shops, then the DVD store, you enter, a score of people browse through the movie aisles, four TV screens all broadcast the same picture, you find the sports section, for a long time you look at DVDs on hockey, baseball, car racing, then you take first one, then another and another still, and since your two hands aren't enough to carry them all, you fetch a basket and you fill it, the cashier flashes a big smile, asks if you won the lottery, but getting no response he doesn't insist, thirteen hundred dollars, all on your credit card, you head out of the store with two full bags, one in each hand, the snow has stopped, you walk for some twenty minutes, you take an overpass, stop in the middle, set the bags down on the ground, lean over the railing, an expressway eight metres below, cars racing by, you pull out the first DVD, hold it over the drop and let go, it falls between two cars and is crushed in under a second, you pull out a second DVD that you throw, this time it bounces off the hood of a jeep, then a third DVD, a fourth, a fifth, you throw them all onto the expressway, one by one, some cars swerve, slam on the brakes, but that's all, you still have a dozen movies left when a voice shouts at you, a pedestrian, a man in his fifties, outraged, he asks you what you think you're doing, he tells you you could cause an accident, so you throw a DVD at him, the man jumps back, a look of stupefaction on his face, then you throw a second one, the man hurries off, yelling that you're a nutcase, and you turn back to the railing and throw your last DVDs onto the expressway, increasingly feverish, you yank your wallet from your pocket, you pull out your local gym membership, you throw it into the void, then your other cards follow, business cards for your sports gear store, health insurance, social insurance, driver's license, Petro-Points, Air Miles, you throw them all out except your bank card and your credit card, then you stumble upon two pictures, one of your wife and the other of your two children, you stare at them for a long, long time, you bite your lip, your eyes fill with tears, but you stretch your hand out toward the void, you spread your fingers and the two pictures flutter for a second before gliding down, like two dried leaves falling from a tree, but you don't watch them fall to the ground, you turn on your heel and away, you walk aimlessly for a while, hunger has set in but you don't think of eating, finally you sit on a snow-covered bench, your hands in your coat pockets, you feel a piece of paper in your pocket and pull it out, that girl Mélanie's address, you think, you stand, hail a passing taxi, give him the address, the taxi starts up, the driver is Haitian and in fine form, talking non-stop, commenting on the mild winter, forever smiling, you say nothing for a moment then you ask him in an expressionless voice how he can be in such good humour after what happened in his country of origin a month and a half ago, the Haitian's serenity instantly evaporates, silence, uneasy glances at his rearview mirror, then his voice sounding

    – It's . . . terrible what happened over there, I know, sir, but . . . What do you want me to do?

                                  pitiful, and you, hearing those words, you nod, you

    – You're right there . . . Anyways, your indifference is probably the best way to tell him to bugger off . . .

                            mutter slowly, and the driver, hearing you, asks who you mean, but you don't answer, the driver says he has no idea what you're talking about, insists he is not at all indifferent to the plight of his people, you just stare outside in silence, gently massaging your sore ribs, ten minutes, you've arrived, back in yesterday's working-class neighbourhood, you recognize Le Losange two blocks away, you're across from a five-storey building, a sign on the door reads "Apartments for Rent, Contact Suite 1," you walk inside, a list of tenants with a mail slot by each name, no buzzers, you go to the inside door and give a push, it isn't locked, you check your piece of paper, go up three flights, door 7, you knock, no answer, you sit down on the floor for a minute then, you lean against the wall, you think, finally you get to your feet, take the stairs down, out on the sidewalk you look around, weary, worn-out, you read the sign on the door a second time, then you go back into the building, over to door number one, knock, a woman in her thirties with furrowed skin and a rasping voice, she's the landlady, there are two apartments for rent, a semi-furnished two-bedroom for the year and a furnished one-bedroom by the month, you visit the one bedroom on the third floor, rickety furniture, grimy oven and fridge, misshapen mattress, creaking bed, you say it's perfect, you take it then and there for a month, five hundred dollars, you pay cash, then you stock up at the supermarket, canned goods, frozen fries, mounds of chips, a case of beer, everything for two hundred and fifty dollars, back to your apartment, you put the food away in the freezer and in the cupboards with their peeling paint, you remove your suit jacket, you open a beer, take a few swigs as you lie down on your bed, then you drop off almost immediately, shifting dreams of your children and wife falling into nothingness, the sound of footsteps on the stairs awakens you, six thirty, your beer has spilled onto the floor, you go to the door, you look through the peephole, you recognize Mélanie climbing the stairs, you hesitate for a second then you step out, you greet her, she stops halfway, she recognizes you, she's stunned, she's happy, even reassured, she comes down to you and explains that, as it happens, she's just come from Le Maquis where she hoped to see you again, then she asks what you're doing in that apartment, you tell her, again she's surprised, you explain that you'll never go back to your house, just as you'll never go back to Le Maquis, she nods her head gravely, silence, then Mélanie smiles, says again how glad she is to see you, on impulse she invites you over for dinner at her place, just like that, you accept indifferently, almost absentmindedly, she needs to get ready, you may come up in an hour's time, finally you notice that her jeans are old and paint-spattered and that her face sports a few yellow spots as well, you return to the apartment, head for the bathroom and peer at yourself in the mirror, your white shirt, your black pants, your three-day stubble, your unkempt hair, you eye the shower, thoughtful, then in the end you leave the room, open a beer and drink it sitting on the couch, you do nothing, you wait, seven thirty, you go up to the fourth floor, Mélanie has had a shower, Mélanie is wearing clean clothes, Mélanie is cooking pasta, you scan the apartment vacantly, threadbare furniture, simple decorations, three movie posters on the walls, *Titanic, Pretty Woman, Amélie,* she asks if you would like something to drink, yes, a beer, she brings you one, you both have a seat in the living room, you're surprised she's not drinking but she shakes her head, evasive, maybe later, she notices the small bruise on your cheek, asks you what happened, you say it's nothing, silence, the bubbling of the pasta cooking, you look around, two generic paintings, framed and sitting on the floor in a corner, Mélanie follows your gaze, she clucks, she says she's been wanting to hang them for weeks now and always comes up with some reason not to, you don't respond, silence, Mélanie doesn't take her eyes off you, as though expecting something, you rub your nose, you set your empty bottle down on the table then, you stand up then, you take two steps then in the direction of the door intending to leave, but Mélanie chooses that moment to return to her stove and cry out with exaggerated enthusiasm that it's ready, so you take a seat almost reluctantly at the table, you both eat, spaghetti and meat sauce, you make no comment about the food, Mélanie apologizes for not having any wine, silence, then you state, your mouth full, that you don't know why you accepted her invitation, she isn't upset by your comment, she even seems happy with the turn the conversation has taken, she swallows her food before

    – Because you know we can help each other . . .

        answering, your face twitches in annoyance, you race through the meal, you say that's not it at all, you're only here because you want to sleep with her, I know you're just trying to provoke her, shock her, but her lips stretch into a sad smile, her fork twisting the spaghetti, a couple of bites, not a hint of irony or

    – You don't wanna go back to your store, you don't wanna go back home . . . Just erase it all, is that it? You

don't want a single tie left to your old life . . . You think that's the answer?

accusation in her voice, so you ask her point blank if she's done this often, hung around bars to pick up poor wretches in the hope of helping them, this time your words seem to affect her, this time she looks down, says no, it's just that she, too, is suffering, she reminds you that you yourself could tell as much last night, she has experienced great misfortune and it has opened her eyes to all kinds of things, to people, all of a sudden you start to panic, you interrupt her, you raise your hand, you warn her that you don't want to know what happened to her, other people's misfortunes don't interest you, you haven't asked her for a single thing, but Mélanie isn't offended, she nods, understanding, she clarifies, choosing her words

– Me either, I don't want to hear your story, but one thing's for sure, misfortune brings us together, we can help each other. I've already started to help myself. You know what I did today?

carefully, but you jump to your feet, remind her that you're not interested, thank her brusquely for supper, head for the door, then it's Mélanie's turn to get up, a tad concerned, she wants to know what your plans are for the evening, you say you're going to a bar, she wrings her hands, suddenly timid, she asks if she can go along, you look undecided, say you don't know, that you want to find someone to fuck, her or someone else, more provocation, you detect pity in her eyes, she says she understands, she understands your attitude, she understands that you're still angry, but you shake your head with a sardonic grimace, tell her it's not anger, tell her it's worse, silence, she says again that she has no desire to sleep with you but she wants to be with you, you tell her you're leaving right now, she pulls on her coat, the two of you step outside, it's really cold out now, you walk toward Le Losange but Mélanie doesn't want to go there, she'd rather be someplace where no one knows her, Mélanie would rather remain anonymous, you shrug, indifferent, you tell her you don't have a car anymore, she doesn't ask any questions and offers to take hers, you climb into her little green Honda Civic, you stare outside in silence, the other cars, the shop windows, but above all the people, your eyes follow them for a long time, you want to go to a nightclub, Mélanie doesn't much feel like dancing, you point out curtly that she shouldn't bother following you then, end of story, she stays quiet for a moment, says she knows a club that's popular with people other than teens, fifteen minutes, stop, then into the dark establishment, blaring rock music, not many people yet, a deserted dance floor, head for the bar, you order a beer without asking Mélanie what she would like, she orders the same, a few sips in silence, the bass makes the floor vibrate, the other patrons are in their thirties or late twenties, thirty minutes, already four beers downed, you start feeling drunk, a 90s hit sweeps through the room, you want to dance then, you practically order Mélanie to follow you, she complies showing neither pleasure or displeasure, you both end up on the dance floor, and you shimmy, and you shake, and you play air guitar, Mélanie's dancing is more restrained, she watches you with a sad gentle smile, three other dancers join you on the dance floor, two women and a man, all a bit younger than you, and you wave your arms wildly, and you close your eyes, and you don't open them even once in fifteen minutes, until Mélanie whispers in your ear that she's going back to sit at the bar, your chance to look around, more people than before, five dancers on the dance floor, and you dance even harder, and you close your eyes again, and you thrash about for another thirty minutes, finally exhaustion sets in, you're winded, you stop, your hands on your thighs, deep breaths, hair pasted to your forehead with sweat, drenched shirt, now there are over a dozen dancers surrounding you, including a girl, early thirties, cute, a good dancer, you sidle over and literally shout that you'd love to sleep with her, she stares, gives an incredulous laugh then turns her back on you, but you insist, but you take her arm, but you ask her what she has to say, and she wants you to leave her alone, she wants you to let go, she wants to get away, and the guy with her finally steps in, he asks you what you think you're up to, you explain that all you want is to screw his friend, but the guy doesn't find it funny, the guy stares you down, the guy orders you to back off, and you confront him full of

 - *It's gotta be fifteen years since my last fight, but I'm sure it'll all come back to me in no time! I gotta say, I like the idea!*

arrogance, the guy looks puzzled then, he must think he couldn't win against you, you're smaller than he is but more built, so he gives a nervous laugh instead then turns his back on you, but you grab his shoulder, but you jerk him round to face you, but you punch him in the nose, and the guy reels, loses his balance, falls to the floor, confusion among the dancers, the girl's cries, your right foot connecting with the guy's ribs, your foot raised for a second go, but arms pull you back, Mélanie's arms, Mélanie telling you to stop, but you push her away, kick him twice more as he lies moaning on the floor, then you stop, you moisten your lips convulsively, the patrons circling you, worried hostile expressions, the girl sobbing hysterically, two customers head toward you with fire in their eyes, their intentions couldn't be clearer, but Mélanie grabs your arm again, tells you you've got to leave right away, you walk to the exit then, outside, you pace back and forth snickering, Mélanie appears a minute later, she's got your coat, you put it on, open wide your arms as you breathe in the cold night air, literally

— *Damn! How did I go without that for so long!*

exulting, Mélanie tells you your attitude leads nowhere but you cut her off roughly, nothing happened to you so she can stop her lecturing, Mélanie sighs, Mélanie runs a hand through her hair, Mélanie says she's going home, and you retort that she can do whatever the fuck she wants, you're going to another club, you start walking,

you hear her behind you begging you not to do
anything stupid, so you turn and your cries engulf the

- What does that mean?! Nothing!

dark street, you stride off, Mélanie's voice still behind
you telling you that tomorrow morning she's going
someplace, she'd like you to go with her, she could
pick you up at nine, but you don't say a word, you keep
walking with the confidence of a soldier entering
conquered territory, your coat undone, impervious to
the biting cold, you pass several bars but it's a
nightclub you want, finally you find one, step inside,
leave your coat at the coat check, an almost full room,
the average age around twenty-two, several people
look at you like you're a dinosaur, you couldn't care
less, you even return their gaze with an arrogance of
your own, you head for the bar, one beer, then another,
lots of pretty young girls, fifteen minutes during
which you drink and watch, then you zero in on a girl,
over there, on the dance floor, twenty-three tops, not
particularly beautiful, a bit plump, but the way she
dances, but the sway of her hips, but her sensual gaze,
you cannot take your eyes off her, over the next ten
minutes two twenty-year-olds sidle up to her, and she
brushes them off jeering, she keeps dancing alone,
undulating her pelvis suggestively, you order a shooter
then, down it and head onto the dance floor, next to
her, you dance up close, the girl notices, the girl looks
surprised, the girl smiles, then she turns her back, not
to ignore you but to thrust her butt toward your pelvis,
rubbing languorously, your hands on her hips, moving

as one, she looks at you over her shoulder, flashing a knowing smile, she turns to face you, places both arms on your shoulders, you exchange a few words as you dance, you learn her name is Andréane, she comes here occasionally but generally speaking guys her age don't interest her, all of a sudden you kiss her full on the lips, she stiffens for a fraction of a second, then laughs, grinds her hips against yours, the two of you keep grinding and dancing for twenty minutes, music, lights, sweat, desire, then she murmurs in your ear that she has to work tomorrow morning, she has to go home early, you say you'll see her home, she giggles, whispers that you certainly don't waste any time, less than thirty minutes later you enter her apartment together, you're so drunk you're reeling, she leads you by the hand to her bedroom, a small bedside lamp sheds subdued light, a clock reads shortly after midnight, a boxspring and mattress lie on the floor, a desk strewn with paper, a small glass table covered in glass knick-knacks, you kiss, excitement rising, clothes falling to the floor, fully nude, you have an incredible erection, you both topple onto the mattress, you caress her, you pant, but you get to your feet, say you need to visit the bathroom, that it will only take a minute, Andréane laughs as you cross the apartment in the dark, you find the bathroom, have trouble urinating because of your erection, then hurry back to the bedroom, you walk over to the mattress on which Andréane still reclines, Andréane reaches for a drawer, Andréane pulls something out of the drawer, a condom, it's a condom, and the sight of the rubber stops you in your tracks, you stand by the mattress, confounded, then you spit out that there is no way you're using that, she frowns, put off by your reaction, but she gives a nervous laugh to try to defuse the situation, says she may be young but she's not reckless, you assure her that you're "safe," that you've been sleeping with the same woman for nine years, but she won't budge, she's not willing to take the slightest risk, she's still smiling but her impatience is starting to show, she makes as though to rip open the envelope but you lean over, tear it from her hands and throw it at

- *That thing's pointless! It's all an illusion! A lie!*

the wall, this time she's stopped smiling, this time she gets up on her elbows, this time she too is angry and tells you you've had too much to drink, you'd best leave, you blink then, giggle idiotically and you stammer an apology, you fetch the condom and you return to the mattress saying you will use it, fine, no problem, you even start to bend toward the mattress, but Andréane pushes you away, decrees that it's too late now, you've spoiled the mood, she accompanies her words with a small cold bitter laugh, avoiding your eyes, and you stand there motionless for a moment, and you stare at her, lying right there, naked, and your erection has disappeared, your penis dangling between your thighs, you nod scornfully then and ask if she thinks that's the way things work, finally she looks at you, she's puzzled, she doesn't understand, you tear into her, she thinks she can bring a guy home just like that, and if things don't go her way, too bad for him, he can just leave, his tail between his legs, isn't that right, she sits up on her elbows, glares, she tells you again to go, it's an order this time, but there's no stopping you now, standing above

- *You think you're stronger than anyone else? That you've got more rights? Did ya ever think that some day, things just might not go your way? That things can't always go the way we want 'em to? Like you might bring a maniac home one night? What about that? What if I was just that, a maniac? A psycho? What would you do then, eh?*

her, but Andréane has had enough, Andréane tries to get up, but you give her a violent push, she falls back, outraged, starts to get up calling you a bastard, a frustrated bastard, so you give it to her, a swift slap, across the face, she falls back a second time, and this time she says nothing, this time she feels her cheek, this time she stares at you in terror, lying on her back, and you mimic surprise, you hiss in a grotesque singsong, oh! that was unexpected, eh, totally unexpected, she has no idea what's about to happen now, the little tease, does she, and the girl starts to scream, the girl calls for help, her screaming makes you wince in annoyance, prompts your hand to grope toward the desk, spurs you to grab the first thing your fingers encounter, the bedside lamp, you drag it toward you, the power cord stretches, pops out of the wall, the room is plunged in darkness, Andréane's screams increase two-fold, fucking screams, screams that might very well be an echo of those uttered by your wife and children in their final moment, is that why her screaming drives you out of your mind, is that why you clamp your free hand over one ear, why you raise the lamp above Andréane yelling at her to shut her trap or you'll hit her, she stops screaming, she sobs, but you're still brandishing the lamp, you bellow you could shatter her skull with it, then what would she do, hey, what could she do, had she ever even thought about that, she begs you not to, and you throw the lamp at a wall, and cast around you, like a man rabid and blind, and you grab hold of the glass table, hoist it up, the knick-knacks fall to the floor, a shrill tinkling like a rain of crystal, and you resume your position above Andréane, your legs planted on the mattress on either side of her body trembling in terror, brandishing the glass table above her, you shout to drown out her sobs and her entreaties, you

- *Or how 'bout the table. That'd be worse! Ever thought of that? The thing is, will I do it? Hey? Who can say one way or another? Who? Not you, not me! No one! Specially not him! Specially not th . . .*

shout yourself hoarse, but panic releases her legs all of a sudden, she kicks out blindly, whimpering, her right leg strikes your left knee, a cry of pain, loss of balance, a fall sideways, your hands slacken, an attempt to regain your balance, but you catch yourself just in time on the desk, you manage to stay on your feet, a sudden silence in the room, no more sobs or cries, your eyes turn to the mattress, Andréane's silhouette in the darkness, a motionless silhouette, and the dark shape covering her face, the table, the small glass table that you let fall involuntarily as you tried to regain your balance, you rush to the wall, hit your shin on a chair, grope for a switch, flick it on, a lightbulb on the ceiling vomits its garish light across the room, now you see everything so clearly, Andréane's bloody face littered with glass shards from the shattered table, a myriad of cuts including two deep ones on her forehead and another large one across her throat, all the blood seeping silently, and worst of all the stillness, total and immutable stillness, you open and close your mouth several times, you draw near, you bend over, take her wrist, check for a pulse, let her hand drop, then you straighten up, you moan, slowly you place your hands on your head and you remain there for long minutes, your features twisted into a hideous mask of terror, an expression unlike anything I have ever seen on your face before, finally you begin to move again, you sprint out of the bedroom, you head for the front door, you open it, you look left and right, a deserted residential street, the neighbouring balconies empty, the other apartment windows in darkness, you shiver with cold, you're still naked, you close the door and return to the bedroom, you pull on your pants looking all the while at Andréane, you put on your shirt your eyes never straying from the body, you slip on your socks your gaze locked still on the corpse, your breathing slow but laboured, your jaw clenched, you leave the room, wander through the dark apartment, and finally, sighing, you drop onto the couch, your arms dangling between your legs, you remain motionless, waiting, resigned, then you drift off to sleep, a dreamless sleep, you open your eyes, sunshine through the windows, you frown and get up, the wall clock reads seven thirty, you look around, dubious, then you return to the bedroom, Andréane's body still there, doubly lit by the lightbulb and the sunlight, the blood no longer flowing, the blood has dried, you return to the hallway, your bafflement grows, you pull on your boots, open the front door, take a few steps onto the balcony, biting cold but magnificent sunshine, you lean against the wrought iron railing, two passersby ignore you, a car motors by, you observe it all with astonishment, then steps can be heard coming down the stairs, a man from the apartment above walks by, barely spares you a glance, you say hello, your eyes full of defiance, and he mumbles a sleepy greeting in return, without slowing down, reaches the street and walks away, you follow him with your eyes for a good long while until he disappears at the end of the street, you look around once more, stand there, your hands on your hips, your head cocked to the left, a few folks on the sidewalks, cars, the day-to-day, you let out a snicker then both incredulous and brazen, return to the apartment, grab your coat from the floor, slip it on and without a glance backward at the bedroom, you step outside, take the stairs, walk down the street, stare insistently at each person you pass, then you stop for a quick breakfast in a café, seemingly lost in thought, dreaming, then a taxi, stop back in front of your new place, you walk into your apartment and sit down on your lopsided couch, motionless, pensive, twenty minutes, a knock on the door then, you turn to the door then, you nod slowly then, both resigned and disappointed, as though knowing it couldn't have lasted, so you walk to the door with a heavy tread, you open it, but you're so surprised to see Mélanie that you look past her to make sure there is no one else, she asks you what's happening, you utter a sound that is as much a snicker as a groan and say, that's just it, nothing's happening, silence, she looks at you, silence, slowly you state that she has no idea what you did last night, but she doesn't want to know, she shakes her head, quickly she switches subjects reminding you she has somewhere she wants to take you today, you ask where, she says you'll see, you make a face and yet you agree, and she says she'll give you ten minutes to get ready but you say you are ready, she looks surprised, she stares at you, dirty hair, shaggy beard, rank, wrinkled clothing, but she makes no comment, she herself is wearing her paint-spattered pants, so you grab your coat, you follow her, you get into her car, the two of you drive in silence for a good long while then finally you speak, without looking at her, you tell her that if she knew what you did last night, she wouldn't want to help you anymore, but she brushes your comment off with a careless wave, reiterates that it isn't just you she wants to help but herself as well, that's what you have to understand, she insists, but her words bring you no comfort, you squirm in your seat, you grimace, you look unwell, you mutter it would be better if you got out here, but she tells you you're almost there, you're somewhere in the east part of the City, faded buildings and stores, some of them dilapidated, the Honda turns down a small street ending in a cul-de-sac, then you stop, a large two-storey house, exterior walls bearing black marks, like burns, you walk toward the front door, the yard is strewn with all kinds of debris, shards of window glass, charred planks, various tools, you step over the threshold, a large room undergoing renovations, four or five people, adult men and women, busy painting, patching, hammering, pop music coming from a CD player in the corner, most everyone greets Mélanie and smiles, and Mélanie greets most everyone and smiles, she asks where Father Léo is, a guy plastering a hole in a wall tells her he's in his office, Mélanie walks to the stairs, but you hesitate, don't budge, reluctant in front of all these people, so she returns to take your hand and guide you, her touch makes you start, but you don't pull your hand away, you follow her, you climb the stairs and arrive at another smaller room, more people working, here the renovations are further along, lively, garish colours, posters showing current movies, bands, stars, Mélanie takes you into a small room at the back, two men consult a plan spread out on the desk, one of them is older, in his sixties, in black clerical dress, a Roman collar, Mélanie approaches, you drop her hand but follow, the priest looks up, greets Mélanie, happy, smiling, tells her the living room is almost done, Mélanie takes in the room and comments on how great it looks, the young people will love hanging out here, the man with the priest walks away, then Mélanie introduces you, his name is Léo, Father Léo, she tells the man of the Church that she met you recently and wanted to show you all this, Father Léo shakes your hand warmly, looks you right in the eye, asks if you've come to join the group, you give a feeble handshake, say nothing, wary, so Mélanie adds she hasn't yet explained what goes on here, the priest nods without taking his eyes off you, an incredibly kind gaze, then someone calls for him from an adjoining room, he excuses himself, leaves the office, you stare at Mélanie, a question, almost an accusation, in your eyes, finally she explains, this group of volunteers has been working for the past two months to rebuild the Youth Centre that burned down last summer, it was the only place where underprivileged youth in the neighbourhood could get together, but the government refused to put any money toward renovating the house, so Father Léo's group sprang into action, the group took over the renovations, everything is done on a volunteer basis, but you have trouble understanding, you ask what the group is exactly, Mélanie adopts a respectful admiring tone, full of compassion, a couple of years ago Father Léo created a sort of association to welcome anyone suffering or striving to give meaning to his or her life, the group always gets involved in community projects, always for society's outcasts, always on a volunteer basis, like last year when the group launched a huge fund-raising campaign to help out the library in a school for severely disabled children, you listen but your wariness remains, your wariness grows, you ask Mélanie how long she has been a member of the association, she says she's known about the group for several months, that she came from time to time but always hesitated to become truly involved and it's only over the past few days that she has genuinely participated, all of which is spoken with

    – In just three days, you can't imagine the good it's done me . . . Not that it's wiped out my suffering, it's just shown me that . . . that suffering isn't my only purpose, that I can do more . . .

                                        glowing pride, then your wariness turns to disdain, your tone scornful, if she thinks you have any intention of joining the group, she's wasting her time, and as you head back downstairs, you hear her ask what you will do with your suffering, but you don't answer, you reach the bottom, you cross the large room, then you stop a second, observe with sullen curiosity the people at work, their serenity, these people who wave politely before returning to the task at hand, then you feel a presence behind you, you turn, it's Father Léo, still smiling, he asks if you too are suffering, actually, it's more an assertion than a question, you shoot back a question of your own, what does he know about it, but he doesn't back down, he says it's plain to see, and that's surely why Mélanie brought you here, you say nothing, out of the corner of your eye you see Mélanie coming down the stairs with another man, both of them carrying a desk, you point out you barely know her but the priest says that's immaterial, and his voice is a

– Knowing each other doesn't matter, recognizing each other is what counts. All people suffering intensely recognize each other.

babbling brook, peaceful and reassuring, and Mélanie sets the desk down, Mélanie turns her head to you, gives her customary smile, where sadness and gentleness meet, you look away then, avoid Father Léo's eyes, then you walk to the door and outside, aimless wandering, mired in your murky thoughts, one hour, two, the streets bustling on a Saturday lunch hour, a crowd parts before you, flows around you like a current around debris, you walk into a fast food joint, three hamburgers, two orders of fries, two soft drinks, return onto the streets slick with black slush, mild temperatures, the sky overcast, this time you have a destination in mind, you look for certain streets, find them, stop often, hesitate, start up again, then finally you recognize yesterday's neighbourhood, your stride confident now, reach a residential street, duplexes and triplexes everywhere, but the closer you get to the apartment, the slower you go, tormented, you notice three patrol cars in the distance, one blocking the street, you approach the perimeter, two cops are stopping people from going any closer, three curious bystanders watch from nearby, staring at Andréane's apartment, people coming and going, likely detectives, serious, grim-looking men, you come to a standstill next to the onlookers, carefully observe the two cops as they stop passersby, but they pay no attention to you, blasé, indifferent, finally you ask what happened, your voice sounding strange, too shrill, one of the cops says he can't say, one of the onlookers tells you there must have been a fatality, he saw a stretcher taken out earlier on, you turn to the cop again and insist, as though

   – *Is it a murder then?*

                              challenging him, but the officer repeats wearily that he can't say, and you keep on staring at him, as though your eyes could convey a message, but he ignores you, casts a bored look round, you nod then, you turn on your heel then, you take off then, seventy minutes, back to your new neighbourhood, you head straight for Le Losange, you're the only customer, you settle in at a table, drink one beer, then another, a few other customers dribble in over the course of the afternoon, you don't even look at them, you don't look at anything, nothing at all, at six o'clock the server's shift is over and she's replaced by another waitress, from the other night you recognize Guylaine, who seemed to know Mélanie, you eye her up and down for a minute, lost in thought, she glances your way as she prepares her cash float, gives you a vague smile, not that she has recognized you necessarily, you take a sip of your third beer, indifferent to the four or five other customers looking as lonely as you, and suddenly in comes Mélanie, she isn't wearing her work pants anymore, she sees you,

she's happy, she comes over to sit at your table, you let
her sit down without saying a word, she'd been to your
place, saw you weren't in, thought you might be here,
you still say nothing, then she invites you out for
dinner but to a restaurant this time, nearby, oh,
nothing fancy, she doesn't have much money, she's
been on welfare for months now, but the food is good,
the atmosphere friendly, and you shoot her a puzzled
look, you toy with the idea, you shake your head, and
yet you accept, making a show of indifference but you
still accept, Guylaine comes up and Mélanie explains
that you're just leaving, the waitress' pout of surprise,
then Mélanie heads for the exit and invites you to
follow, outside night has fallen, just a few minutes
later you enter a restaurant, a modest little place,
gawdy decorations, soppy music, a room half-full, you
take a table at the back, she orders the skewers, you
order a bunch of stuff, way too much, Mélanie looks
at you uncomfortably but says nothing, then she talks
about Father Léo's project, the Youth Centre
renovations are coming along nicely, within a week's
time everything should be ready, she's excited,
passionate, elated, you listen wordlessly, the meals
arrive, you eat, she keeps talking about her group of
volunteers, then asks you why you didn't stay today,
you chew your souvlaki dripping with sauce, you say
it doesn't interest you, she isn't offended, she's
disappointed but not offended, claims that certain
people can be resistant at first, just like she was during
her initial visits a few weeks ago, she only truly started
to get involved a few days ago, but you sigh, you say

it's not the same thing, from the start she was looking for help, whereas you aren't looking, you're not looking for any help, you're not looking for anyone, and your voice is curt, your voice is harsh, your voice carries on propelled by its own lack of resonance, Mélanie responds that you just think you're not looking for anything, you take a sip of the cheap wine you ordered, mutter as you ask why she wants to help you so badly, then she says again that she's doing it for herself too, like all the people you saw this morning at the Youth Centre, they too are doing it as much for themselves as for the underprivileged youth, that's what you have to understand, but you've already finished eating, you swipe at your mouth with the back of your hand, staining the sleeve of your increasingly worse-for-wear shirt, state with a certain tone of aggression that you don't want any help, but she's not discouraged, and her smile returns, gentle and sad, as

– All the same, you move into my building, go to bars with me and come to dinner with me, even though I won't sleep with you . . .

always, she must notice your irritation because she takes your hand, you give a start, Mélanie says it doesn't matter, Mélanie is patient, Mélanie will wait for your anger to cool, you pull your hand away then, you mutter that if she knew what you'd done last night, she would be a lot less conciliatory, but she doesn't look away, she murmurs that everyone does awful things, you pull a sardonic

- But I don't give a shit what I do.

grimace, she shakes her head slowly, her exasperating smile, and she murmurs one word, one only, "liar," in a breath that brushes your cheek like a metallic feather, you stand up then, she asks where you're going, you say you've finished your meal, there's no reason to stay, she asks if you'd like to go for a drink somewhere, you turn her down curtly, bid her goodbye without thanking her for the meal, start walking toward the door, she says nothing, doesn't try to detain you, you find yourself outside, the temperature surprisingly mild, you walk over tamped-down snow, a furious gait, your jaw clenched, and you stop, and you think for a moment, and you hail a cab, the driver asks where you're going, you give him the name of that dangerous district that's so often in the news, the car starts moving, fifteen minutes, stop at an intersection, you pay the driver, get out, you start walking, you look around you, closed dingy-looking shops, housing bordering on slum dwellings, dim light through windows, the streets quiet even on a Saturday, a few pedestrians here and there who don't even spare a glance for you, ten minutes, then four people, men and women, a small group in front of a bar, you draw near, a brazen expression on your face, they see you coming, walk off, slip into an apartment building, disappointment flits across your face, for a second you contemplate the entrance to the seedy bar then keep on walking, five minutes, two guys farther up exchange something, shoot furtive glances left and right, you draw closer, but they move away as you approach, your exasperation grows, you carry on, pass more indifferent pedestrians whom you stare at insistently in vain, then you stop in the middle of the deserted street, your hands on your hips, your head cocked, the same pose as this morning on Andréane's balcony, and you wait, and you wait, then noise, sounds, an altercation nearby, by that clothing store, you start in that direction, voices coming from out back, you walk around the store, the only light back there comes from a naked bulb on a third-floor balcony, but you can make out silhouettes, five of them, and they're yelling at each other between two buildings' walls, you're a few metres away by now and you study them intently, you manage to deduce that three Latinos are arguing with two white guys, they're discussing drugs, rates, they're young, twenty at the most, and there's a girl with the white guys standing off to the side, silent, subdued, then one of the Latinos finally spots you and asks what the fuck you're doing, the guys stop talking, the guys stare at you, but the guys look a bit frightened too, you keep your answer short, you say you're defying logic, the Latino who spoke approaches then and the others follow suit, they've forgotten their fight, the girl takes a few steps too, you examine her attentively, the girl who's still just a teen, fifteen or sixteen, pretty but looking so indifferent, and without meaning to your eyes fill with despair, and without meaning to you murmur words that

– Would Béatrice have turned out like you some day?

you seem to regret almost instantly because you rub your face furiously, you turn your eyes back to the gang, especially the Latino, up close by now, studs in his nose and eyebrows, his worn leather jacket, gel spiking his short hair, his expression striving for menace but still oozing childhood, he asks if you're looking for trouble, and you shrug, you say it doesn't matter what you're looking for, you might not find it, what's supposed to happen doesn't necessarily happen, and more of

– Like last night . . . Like tonight . . . How can you know?

the same, the other guys shoot each other a puzzled look, and then the Latino closest to you pulls a revolver out of the pocket of his jacket, the Latino points the weapon some fifty centimetres from your face, the Latino says you'd better bugger off, and quick, but he's nervous, but he's trembling slightly, and you stare at the weapon for a second, expressionless, you state that logically you should run away, of course, but since logic is useless, the question is what will end up happening, they don't get it, nerves, tension, the armed Latino cocks the hammer, moistens his lips, tells you again to clear off, you grab the wrist of his raised hand, you pull him toward you then, until the barrel of the gun rests against your forehead, and the Latino's eyes grow wide, horrified, and he stammers that he'll shoot if you don't let go, yes, he'll shoot, hear that, he'll gun you down, but his voice lacks conviction, fear has taken up all the space, you squeeze his wrist even tighter then, the Latino squeals in pain, drops the weapon that bounces off the ground, and they scatter, every man for himself, including the girl, including the Latino who threatened you, they bolt, they disappear into the night, once or twice you hear a "fucking psycho" in the distance, then silence, the firearm on the ground glowing in the light of the naked bulb, your eyes curious, your hands scoop up the revolver, close inspection of the weapon, the cylinder that you eventually open, two out of six chambers loaded, and that fact brings a glint to your eye, a sudden illumination, you spin the cylinder then, close it again, cock the hammer and place the barrel against your temple, and you hold your breath, and you don't hesitate, and you squeeze the trigger, a click, that's all, no gunfire, you observe the revolver with satisfaction then, slide it awkwardly into your pants, under your coat, start walking again, back to the street, fifteen minutes, you've left the neighbourhood, seventy-five minutes, you walk by the fast food joint where you abandoned your car the other night, you notice the car's still there, you continue, twenty-five minutes, you recognize your new neighbourhood, you find an open convenience store, you buy a bottle of cheap wine, the sales clerk at the counter tells you the price, you stare at him for a long minute, you reach toward your pants, for the gun, but you end up pulling out some bills and you pay, you notice you have about fifty dollars left, outside, bank, cash machine, you insert your bank card but a message pops up telling you you cannot withdraw any funds from this account, you try another account, same message, you stare at the screen for a long while, you insert your credit card, hoping for a cash advance, but a message tells you that the card is no longer valid, you sigh, leave, look for another bank, try another machine, same scenario, same refusal, you grit your teeth, punch and crack the screen, you hurt your hand, just a bit, you leave, outside, five minutes, your building, the stairs, the door to your apartment, you swing it open, but on your way inside you glance toward the stairs, toward the steps up to the next floor, you chew on your lip, I'm sure that part of you wants to climb the stairs, but in the end you enter your own apartment, you lay the revolver down on the kitchen table, then nothing, hesitation, thinking, then you frown as though at your own idiocy, and you leave your apartment, the bottle in hand, you climb the stairs, it's eleven o'clock but there's still light coming from under the door, you knock, Mélanie opens the door almost immediately, not in her pyjamas, Mélanie's still dressed, Mélanie is happy, reassured, Mélanie invites you inside and you comply like a slightly shamefaced mutt, you find yourself in the living room, the bottle of wine open, you each drink a glass, the TV's on but you both ignore it, then Mélanie asks if you'd like to go back to the Youth Centre with her tomorrow, a second chance, and you don't answer, you notice once more the modest decor, the pastel colours, the framed paintings still on the floor in the corner of the room, and Mélanie repeats her question, all of a sudden you ask her to lend you some money, she seems surprised, you explain that your bank accounts have been frozen, your credit card too, because you haven't been in touch with anyone for three days now, because you owe the funeral home, your family must have asked the police to freeze your accounts to force you to resurface, they must know you're in Montréal since you paid for some DVDs with your credit card and they must imagine you're wandering around aimlessly in a state of shock, they're convinced the lack of funds will force you to return in short order, Mélanie listens, her legs tucked beneath her, glass in hand, then she says they could be right, you get annoyed then, it's not at all like that, she hasn't understood a thing, you're not in a state of shock, you're not wandering aimlessly, you're waging a war, and Mélanie asks against whom, but you don't answer, you drain your glass, you pour yourself another, Mélanie suggests you go to pay the money owed, reassure everyone, then explain that you don't want to hear from a single soul, and that would be it, you could come back here, but your patience is wearing thin, and as you speak you

    - *I don't wanna go back, not even for a few hours! I don't wanna see anyone again! No one!*

                        thump your thigh, and you finish your glass, then you calm down, ask if she plans to call the cops, she says no, with her sad and gentle smile, says again with compassion that she is here to help you, you hold her gaze, then your lips move, stretch out and up, take the shape of something resembling a smile, I'm not even sure you're aware it's happened, and Mélanie's face lights up as though she'd just received a Christmas present, but serious now, she explains she can't really lend you any money, she's been living on welfare since she lost her cashier's job six months ago, she lowers her eyes then, confesses she used to lead a dissipated life, lots of partying, a lot of irresponsibility, collecting lovers, and suddenly you're listening very closely, but she stops short, her head down, embarrassed, you stare then at the glass you're rolling between your palms, your expression solemn, something hangs there suspended, hovers, quivers, and when you speak your voice is a

   - If you tell me your story, I'll tell you what happened to me too . . .

      whisper, she keeps her eyes down, tormented, her long hair draped on either side of her face, then she lifts her head and asks again if you'll come tomorrow, you drain your glass and pour yourself another, the switch in topics makes you surly, you grunt probably not, you make as though to get to your feet and leave but she points at the TV, where a Hitchcock movie has begun, she says she loves the oldies, she invites you to stay and watch with her, she insists, her big eyes, her sad gentle smile, and you stare at her, your resentment remains, and yet you settle back, and the two of you watch the movie in silence for half an hour, you drink alone, your gaze in the middle distance, scarcely aware of the movie, and at times your eyes glisten with rage, and at others they fill with infinite anguish, at still others they dive down into the abyss, then finally you realize that Mélanie has fallen asleep, you get to your feet, you look at her for a long time, your eyes admiring her body, her legs in their form-fitting jeans, her pretty yet sad face even in sleep, then finally you do walk to the door, the half-finished bottle in your hand, your apartment, your couch, alone, you drink the rest of the bottle, then you do nothing for a while, you put on your coat then, slide the gun into your pants, leave the apartment, walk to Le Losange, one thirty, only a couple of customers, two men talking at a table, Guylaine now replaced by a vapid, miserable barman, disappointment flits across your face, you sit down alone at another table, half a dozen beers, two forty-five, you're the only one left in the bar, the barman is reading a video game magazine, you toy with the gun under your coat but you don't pull it out, you look out the window, all of a sudden your eyes fill with tears, and you bite your lip so as not to cry, and you pound the table so as not to cry, and you grit your teeth so as not to cry, and when the barman pronounces a weary last call, you stand up, you pay and you leave the bar, you lurch into the street, you come to a standstill, you pull out the revolver, there's a pedestrian down the street, you open the cylinder housing its two bullets, spin it, close it again, then raise the weapon in the direction of the pedestrian, you aim at him for a long time, and he keeps on walking oblivious, crosses an intersection, disappears, then a car passes, you level the gun at it until it too is out of range, then you aim at a window, then finally at the sky, you point at the sky for a long, long time while a broken, barely audible moan dribbles from your lips like snot, then you lower your weapon, then you walk into your building, then you climb the stairs, you enter your apartment, lie down in your bed, fully dressed, your face turned to the ceiling, and you guide the barrel to your temple, but you don't pull the trigger, but you don't budge, but you do nothing, and finally you fall asleep in that position, you dream of Andréane, her screams, her terror, the table dropping onto her face, and you dream of me as well, but in a muddled fashion, then you're awakened by a knock at the door, it's morning, the gun lies on the floor, your head is pounding, you lie there for at least ten minutes, then you get up painfully, the knocking stopped a while back but you make your way to the door anyway, open it, a note on the floor, it's Mélanie, she writes that she knocked but no one answered, she gives the address to the Youth Centre, she invites you to meet her there, you slip the piece of paper into your pocket without thinking, the time is nine ten, you go to the bathroom, fill a glass with water but at the last minute, you decide not to drink it, then you look into the bathroom mirror, your greasy hair, your beard long enough to show several grey hairs, your clothes filthy and stained in spots, you sniff under your arms, you can smell your shirt, you grimace in disgust, yet a certain satisfaction is discernible too, you walk to the living room, boots, coat, revolver, outside, it's snowing, cars inch forward, you head for the closest restaurant, you scarf down three muffins and two cups of coffee, only three other customers, two of whom read the newspaper, an idea seems to cross your mind, you fetch a paper, bring it back to your table, leaf through and finally find on page seven a shortish article explaining that you've disappeared, you were last seen at the funeral home, there's even a small picture of you, smiling, you're barely recognizable, but when the article starts to recount the *tragedy*, you stop and snap the paper shut, then you watch the other two read their papers, no one pays attention to you, you dig through your pockets, a twenty-dollar bill and a few coins, you head for the exit, the girl at the counter calls after you looking for payment but you don't even bother turning around, you step outside, the snow is thicker now, the wind stronger, pedestrians raise their coat collars for protection and you do the same, a long walk, sixty minutes, you're across from Sylvain's duplex, whipped by falling snowflakes, you raise your head to look up at the apartment, reluctant but resigned, you climb the stairs then, you ring the doorbell, Sylvain opens, Sylvain in shock, Sylvain's mouth ajar, and you do nothing, say nothing, stand there, your hands in your pockets, finally Sylvain stammers for you to come in, you comply, doffing neither boots or coat, and in the living room-cum-dining room find a pretty girl in her twenties sitting at the table eating breakfast, she's wearing Sylvain's robe, she greets you shyly, and you recognize the girl from the other day, the day you broke the news to your friend, and you're stunned to see her a second time, but Sylvain draws near, Sylvain takes you by the shoulders, Sylvain asks where you've been, everyone's looking for you, everyone's worried, and you let him talk and when he stops to catch his breath, you make it clear that you hate being here, in this apartment, with him, and Sylvain is speechless, then finally he remembers the girl, stupidly introduces you, her name is Sarah, and her expression, on hearing your name, positively drips with compassion, as though she knew you already, you eye her disdainfully then ask Sylvain since when does he have his flings stay for breakfast, Sarah looks embarrassed, Sylvain flinches but doesn't falter, asks again where you've been, what you've been doing, and he tries to convince you to call your brother, your brother-in-law, your store, everyone, because they're all worried, he keeps on repeating it, he's genuinely distressed, says you need to get a grip and assures you he'll help, and you listen and stare as though he were a creature from another planet, as though he were speaking to you in a foreign language, you interrupt him then, point out that the only reason you're here is to ask for money, but he doesn't understand, how can that be, you have more money in your bank account than he could ever earn in a year, you lose patience then, explain that your accounts have been frozen, and Sylvain says that's understandable, given you're on the run, but he doesn't finish his sentence, you yell that you're not on the run, a brief emotionally-charged silence, then Sylvain takes you by the shoulders again, you stiffen at the unwanted touch, he switches tactics, orders you to sit down, tells you the two of you will talk, there's no rush, but you shrug free stating you're not interested, you don't want to listen to anyone, you don't want a family anymore, relatives or friends, and you're sweating in your coat, and you sigh, and you take a few steps back, Sylvain is bewildered, Sylvain says he's there for you, he's still your friend, but you say no, that too is over, you say again just how difficult it was for you to come, you're only here for the money, end of story, Sylvain's expression changes then, despair and frustration, he plants his hands on his hips and asks whether you think he won't call anyone, the police, your family, to tell them you're here, in the City, that you've gotten in touch with him, you feel all confused, you scratch your head, so itchy it's as though your scalp harboured colonies of ants, you mutter you didn't expect him to tell anyone about your visit, he barks out a bitter laugh, asks by what right you would think that, but you have no answer, you keep scratching your head, your frigging head, and Sylvain, in a fury born of dismay and helplessness, asks again by what right you would think that, not because of your friendship on which you've turned your back, so why, dammit all, why, and you grimace, you sweat even more, you concede he's right, you should never have come, you make as though to leave, but Sylvain grabs your arm, Sylvain has already forgotten his outburst, Sylvain speaks in a tone of distress, he understands your confusion, your revolt, but it's absurd, they lead nowhere, and his words

- You don't want ties to anything anymore, you don't wanna depend on anything anymore or owe anything to anyone, but c'mon, that can't work! The proof is you need money! You've gotta see you can't just say fuck it all, that won't work!

cause you to moan, as though each syllable pierces your skin, you jerk away and suddenly Sarah intervenes, gently suggests that you listen to your friend, you glare at her then and order her to mind her own business, you turn to Sylvain and ask him since when does he discuss you with his flings, discomfort on Sylvain's part, then he reveals that Sarah isn't just a lover, Sarah's his girlfriend, they've been together for a week or so, but he didn't mention it six days ago, it really wasn't a good time, but you're stunned at the news, dumbfounded, bowled over, you utter then the darkest and most ironic of half-laughs, still scratching your

- So even you! Even you!

scalp as it bleeds lightly under your fingernails, softly Sylvain begs you to be quiet, says you're the one who's been had, by your rage, your despair, your anger, but you don't listen, you ask Sarah if she has any idea what a womanizer her new lover is, how he'd screw anyone anywhere, no ties allowed, again Sylvain tells you to be quiet, his annoyance growing with Sarah's embarrassment, but you continue, or does she know he has a computer full of naked girls, pictures of orgies, does she know he smokes pot almost daily, snorts coke occasionally, has been known to call on escorts when he's got the means, about three or four times a year, and Sylvain yells at you to stop, and you make a beeline for his desk, you open a drawer you know well, you pull out a little bag full of white powder that you throw at Sarah, now Sylvain clenches his hands into fists, now he shouts that's enough, now he shrieks at you to get out, while Sarah hangs her head, rubs her forehead and murmurs two words that

- *My God* . . .

send you over the edge, that have you screaming at her to shut up, that make you slap her full across the face, then Sylvain jumps you, you fling him off, he flies into the wall, shakes himself then grabs his phone, his hands trembling, his voice shaking, he's going to call the cops, he has no choice, you need help, and suddenly you pull out your gun, point it at Sylvain who freezes, his eyes literally crossing as he stares at the weapon, the phone just short of his ear, and you're panting so hard you don't even hear the girl's whimpers, slowly Sylvain puts the phone down, terrified, incredulous, he stammers that you've gone crazy, he begs you to calm down, but slowly you advance, your breath wheezing, your face drenched in sweat, your lips twisted into a horrific smirk, your voice

– This is chaos, Sylvain . . . You'll never get away from it . . . Never . . .

rasping, quick you open the cylinder, quick you make it spin, quick you close it again, and you take aim at Sylvain, who's choked with terror, the barrel sixty centimetres from his face, and your voice is nothing more now

– Chaos and chance . . . Nothing else exists . . .

than a vestige of breath, and you squeeze the trigger, the click of the firing pin fuses with Sylvain's cry, Sarah's screams, then Sylvain falls to his knees, Sylvain lowers his head to the floor, Sylvain erupts into sobs, and Sarah rushes to enfold him in her arms, to cradle him, to wail with him, and you watch the two of them clinging to each other, both of them in tears, and your brow knits, and your bottom lip begins to tremble, and your stomach begins to heave, and suddenly you throw up on the carpet, a single mighty vile stream, no reaction from the sobbing couple, you wipe your mouth with a shaking hand, you slide the weapon back into your pants, you hurry out of the apartment, nearly fall down the stairs in your agitation, it's still snowing heavily, you start to stagger down the sidewalk, stop, rub your eyes hard, give a long, keening moan, but you resume walking, into the wind blowing through your filthy hair, intersection, a commercial street, practically deserted now because of the weather, a taxi does come along finally, you climb into the back, the driver asks where you're off to, you say nothing for a few seconds, dazed, paralyzed, the driver reiterates his question, you shake yourself awake, dig through your pockets, Mélanie's note, the written address, twenty minutes, stop in front of the Youth Centre, barely recognizable through the curtain of continually falling snow, the fare is twenty-three dollars, you give the driver a twenty, explain that's all you have, the driver balks, starts to kick up a fuss, but you scream you don't have any more, the driver stammers okay, finally you get out, climb the rise, walk into the house, find yourself in the same room as yesterday, five people busy working, you spot Mélanie at the back, perched on a stepladder, painstakingly painting a doorframe, so intent on her task she doesn't even notice you, you watch her for a minute, fascinated, then hurry up the stairs, pass a few people, enter Father Léo's office, the priest is there, bent over some papers he's studying, he recognizes you right away, smiles kindly, asks how you're doing, but you start in on him, your voice harsh, your rancour incomprehensible, why do all these people come here, why do they join the group, and gently he answers that the common element here is people's suffering, but his answer only serves to goad you, you ask what they're suffering from, you ask what happened to them, Father Léo clasps his hands in front of him, explains that no one here knows another's suffering, he points at all the people at work

– We're not a discussion group for sharing, we're here to act. Those who join aren't required to explain why they're

*suffering. It doesn't matter. What does matter is doing
something to offset the suffering. Because we are defined
not by what we say but by what we do.*

around him, you're skeptical as you observe him,
still dissatisfied, still tormented, then you return
downstairs, back to the other room, Mélanie still
intent on her work, you watch her from a distance,
your face confused at first, as though a fissure, a crack
was about to open and release something from within,
but finally your features harden and you turn on your
heel, Father Léo is standing there, he has come
downstairs, he has followed you, he looks at you, you
pass him and you spit out your words

- Your boss is a liar and a double-crosser.

without stopping,
he doesn't react but a glimmer of compassion appears
in his eyes, you hurry outside, it's storming now, you
start to walk, your eyes full of snow, reach a major
thoroughfare, a convenience store nearby, you enter,
no customers, the clerk barely looks up from his
iPhone, it doesn't take you long to spot a surveillance
camera behind the counter, you leave immediately,
fifteen minutes by foot to the next corner store, you
enter, tiny interior, a lone customer pays at the
counter, you scan the room for a camera and find
none, you approach the counter, finally the other
customer leaves, the Asian clerk smiles, you pull out
your gun, take aim, demand all the cash in the register,
the sales clerk is nervous but controlled, hurriedly he

gives you all the bills in the register, you stuff them into your coat pockets, then stare at the clerk, still aiming at him, you hesitate, finally you hit him with the grip, he crumples to the floor, moaning, half-stunned, you rush out, you walk through the storm until you find a taxi, during the cab ride you count the money, 140 dollars in all, the taxi stops in front of Le Losange, you pay, step out, walk inside, Guylaine is behind the bar and this time she seems to recognize you, even calling out that you look like a snowman, a lone customer, a woman in her fifties playing the slot machine at the back of the room, you sit by a window, the server approaches, you order a beer, your voice surly, Guylaine walks off, you start thinking then, you look conflicted as though trying to convince yourself that what you're about to ask isn't a good idea, Guylaine returns with the beer, you ask her then what happened to Mélanie, the server doesn't understand, you try to be more specific, you know something terrible happened to Mélanie recently, but you don't know what, Guylaine is surprised, she doesn't know either, she adds that Mélanie has always come across as unhappy, showing up at the bar every night, often to get drunk, but if something serious happened recently, that would explain why she's hardly been by for the past week, then Guylaine returns to the bar, and you drink looking outside, and you stare into the emptiness, and you seem to struggle with conflicting ideas, harrowing thoughts, and the hours pass, and you drink, beer, shooters, two other customers appear, sit down together in a corner, and darkness slowly overtakes the streets, the snowstorm continues, Guylaine brings you your ninth beer, you grab her arm then, ask her what you should do, she gives a start, doesn't understand, and you insist, your voice thick and

- What do I do now? Sit here drinking 'til I've got no money left? Leave and shoot some stranger? Throw myself off some damn bridge? What the fuck do I do?

broken, Guylaine tries to free herself, the first signs of panic showing in her eyes, and just then you see Mélanie through the window, in the snowstorm, crossing the street, walking toward her building, you stand up then, start pounding on the window, pounding so hard she finally turns around, shelters her face from the snow, recognizes you, but Guylaine has had enough, she tells you you should go, Mélanie is already inside the bar, you make your way to her, your gait unsteady, waving your arms with a dramatic flourish, you sneer as you ask whether she's spent another day renovating that frigging house, being the do-gooder, deceiving herself that life has some kind of meaning, the other three customers look at you embarrassed, Mélanie watches you draw near, you stop once you're up close, then she answers, without the slightest trace of irony or

- I'm happy with my day. I feel I've done some good. For me, that's got a whole lotta meaning.

mockery, you hold her gaze but you have nothing to retort, you bite your lip, all of a sudden you retrieve your coat, all of a sudden you head for the exit, and behind you Mélanie's gentle voice, telling you she's there, she will always be there, no matter what you do, you turn to her, her calm, her certainty, her eyes full of compassion sending you into such a fury that you kick at a chair on your way out, in the street, the storm is raging, you look for another taxi, cursing, staggering, swearing at everyone and no one, you find a cab, you give the Youth Centre address, the driver seems concerned by your condition, but he says nothing and begins to drive, he tries to engage you in conversation about the weather, but you don't answer, your crazed eyes staring at your feet, your shaking hands between your knees, a vein throbbing in your temple, stop at your destination, you grab a twenty and a ten that you throw at the driver, step out, struggle up the slight snow-covered rise leading to the front door, slip, fall, get back up, turn the knob, the door opens, a moment's astonishment, as though you expected it to be locked, then you enter, the room empty but the light's on, painting finished, the decorating further along, you roam through the room, turn in circles, sway, look at everything with your crazed eyes, tools, plywood, cans of paint, CD player, a stray pack of cigarettes, old newspapers, forgotten coat, freshly painted walls, new furniture, and your eyes glisten with hatred, and you pick up a hammer leaning against the wall, and you start swinging at the walls, the furniture, breaking, smashing, demolishing, you cry with each blow, so loudly that you don't hear the noise above and on the stairs, too swept away by your fury, and you swing and you swing and you freeze suddenly at the sight of a silhouette framed in the door leading to the hallway, it's Father Léo, one hand against the doorframe, the other down by his side, Father Léo watching you in silence, Father Léo suddenly looking so old, and the only emotion on his face is one of disappointment, nothing more, and your chest is heaving, you are drenched in sweat and melting snow, silence, the howling of the storm, then the priest asks what you're doing here, you drop the hammer then, bury your hand inside your coat, pull out the revolver, and as you open the cylinder, as you spin the cylinder, as you close the cylinder, you answer in a voice by now verging on hysteria, that you are the instrument of chaos, and you raise the firearm and you aim at the priest, your tongue moistens your lips several times, your arm swaying from the effects of the alcohol, your teeth clenched to the point of cracking, but Father Léo doesn't move, he keeps his hand on the doorframe, ignores the weapon, he looks at you, yes, you, and his voice is so slow, so very very

– No, you are not the instrument of chaos. You create chaos. There is a huge difference.

slow, you squeeze the trigger then, a deafening boom, in the room, in your head, everywhere, your arm literally propelled backwards, a flash of pain in your right shoulder, two or three seconds' worth of confusion, then you realize that Father Léo is no longer standing, he's sprawled on the ground, you blink several times, then you draw near, the bloodstain spreading outwards on his white shirt above his solar plexus, his open eyes staring at the ceiling, his left hand opening and closing on the floor, his rattling breath growing weaker and weaker, ten seconds, twenty seconds, then the priest makes no more sound, the priest moves no more, the priest is dead, you stare at him in silence, and slowly a grimace distorts your features, a horrific blend of hatred, appeasement and despair, you return to the room then, pick up the hammer and start raining down blows on everything, punctuated not with your cries this time but with a harsh keening emanating from a darkness from which nothing human can emerge, your fevered eyes fall on the pack of cigarettes on the floor then, you drop the hammer, you pick up the pack and you open it, a matchbook inside, in no time you have lit several matches, you throw them into every pile of paper and sawdust you see, a half-dozen small fires spring to life in the room, you walk toward the front door, you open it, you glimpse a car parked across the street, I imagine you hadn't noticed it earlier on, you return inside then, in two spots the fire has already begun to spread, you step over the priest's body, hurry up the stairs, enter the office, rummage through Father Léo's coat, find his car keys, then you open the top desk drawer, then the second, you come up with a hundred dollars or so, you take the money, head back downstairs, step over

Father Léo again, this time you glance at him briefly, then you cross the room already full of smoke, your gun, where is your gun, you turn in circles, crouch, spit, there, it's on the floor right there, you make your way over, jam it in your coat pocket, finally outside, you tumble down the rise coughing, you climb into Father Léo's car and take off, in your drunkenness your driving is erratic but fortunately the streets are practically deserted, visibility is near zero, skidding, distorted view, a storm raging both inside and outside your head, fifteen minutes, then you skid one too many times, hit a pole, you get out, recognize the neighbourhood, it's not far now, you run then into the wind, whipped by snow, and you reach your building, and you enter and you stumble upstairs, and you bang with all your might on Mélanie's door, she opens it to you, and suddenly she's frightened, as though at the sight of you in this state she knows what is about to happen, you shove her then, you enter and close the door, you grab Mélanie's hand, you drag Mélanie to her room, you push Mélanie onto her bed, Mélanie crumpling onto the mattress, begging you no, panic in her voice, and you strip, without a word, now you're naked, you've got an erection, you order her to strip, but she refuses, still begging you to stop, you mustn't, don't, you mustn't, you swoop down on her then, in a fury you rip off her clothes, she starts to struggle but your fist connects with her left eye, she goes limp then, half-conscious, and you stretch out on top of her, you penetrate her violently, her dryness, a cry of pain, her body stiffens, then your to-and-fro, your savage piston moves, and your grunting, and your lowing, but soon your vigour is lost, and you cry in rage, you intensify both in ardour and violence, but nothing helps, your member too limp now to continue its ravages, you stop then finally, still lying on Mélanie who struggles weakly, your face buried in the mattress by her head, a terrible retching, your stomach turns over, you roll onto your side and finally you founder, shadows, nothingness, perhaps you've passed out, perhaps you're asleep, it doesn't matter, the fall is the same, and when you open your eyes again, sunlight filters through the bedroom's half-open curtains, you sit up on your elbows, splitting pain in your head, sounds from the next room, Mélanie appears, wearing not her workclothes but clean jeans, a woolen sweater, she sets a tray down on the mattress next to you, toast, coffee, a large glass of cranberry juice, two pills, you stare at her stupidly, she stands there, her hands clasped in front of her, her hair tied back in a ponytail, her left eye black and swollen, no reproach in her gaze, no anger, only resignation with perhaps a shadow of hope emerging, finally she speaks, suggesting you wash the pills down with the glass of juice, an even voice, no intonation, and you obey, you swallow the pills, you drink half a glass, docile, the clock on the desk reads nine thirty, Mélanie explains that she didn't want to leave you alone this morning, that she'll go to the Youth Centre this afternoon or tomorrow, you sit up on the mattress, you examine her in silence, incredulous, bewildered, she adds then that she told you, she will be there, she will always be there, no matter what you do, no matter what you've done, you lower your head then, rub your forehead, and you yourself seem surprised to hear the words that

– *I'm sorry . . .*

cross
your dry lips, silence, then a small smile appears on Mélanie's lips, and the hope in her eyes is no longer just a shadow but has taken on a tangible form, real and alive, an incongruous ringing, the telephone, Mélanie leaves the bedroom, you stare at your breakfast then bite into the toast, chew diligently, suddenly a cry from Mélanie, followed by an agitated discussion, then she reappears in the bedroom, beside herself, on the verge of tears, she explains, her words tumbling over each other in her hurry, that was Guy, one of the group members, the Youth Centre was torched again last night, a burned body was discovered in the rubble, perhaps Father Léo, the police don't know yet, now her tears fall, she paces the room, exclaims how terrible, how awful, the project was so important, near completion, and the corpse, Oh, Lord, that corpse, and you look at her, and you are petrified, and you can't swallow the food rotting in your mouth, and for the space of a second Mélanie examines you in shock, as though a grim doubt has just crossed her mind, but she shakes herself, declares she wants to be with the group, share her sorrow with the other members, she leaves the room, you push away the breakfast tray then, fold your knees up close, hug them tight, your face contorted, Mélanie returns,

wearing her coat, anguish, sorrow, but great resolve as well, she says she'll be back in an hour or two, but she already knows what the group's decision will be, she has no

– *We won't stop. We'll start over, that's all. I'm sure everyone'll feel the same. Even if that was Father Léo who died in the fire, it's what he would've wanted: for us to continue.*

doubt in that regard, and her certainty makes her more beautiful than ever, and you stare at her, your mouth ajar, as though her words have paralyzed you, you clear your throat then, you take a big breath then, and your voice

– *If you do start over, I . . . I'll help you.*

trembles, as do your limbs, as does your heart, and it's Mélanie's turn to take a deep breath, Mélanie is moved, Mélanie nods, all suspicion gone from her eyes, finally she turns to go but you call after her, you say that when she comes back, you have something to tell her, so much to tell her, but she turns back toward you, her expression solemn now, she mumbles you need feel no obligation, you say you want to, yes, you want to, Mélanie says nothing, leaves, the banging of the front door, you stay seated on the bed, your face visited by a thousand conflicting emotions, twenty minutes, finally you get up, you wince slightly as you feel the pain in your right shoulder, you stare at your filthy clothes on the floor, you walk to the bathroom and look at yourself in the mirror, your gaze appalled, you turn on the tap then, slide under the shower and close your eyes, you let the water splash over you until it turns cold, finally you wash your body, you wash your hair then you step out, for a moment you contemplate a razor as though thinking of shaving off your beard, but you drop the idea, you return to the bedroom but only pull on your pants, you rummage through Mélanie's drawers, find the biggest T-shirt she owns, plain white, you slip it on, a bit tight but it will do, you find a pair of socks and pull them on, you pick up your coat and head for the living room to drop it on the armchair, but you seem to remember something, you dig through the coat pocket and pull out the revolver, you open the cylinder, there's still one bullet left, you give the weapon a sharp look, then you slide it under your T-shirt, you shrug into your coat, step outside, the snow has stopped, you turn into the alley beside the building, make sure no one is watching, then throw the revolver into a trash can, return to the building, to Mélanie's apartment, to the living room, you sit in an armchair and don't move, one hour, one long hour, sixty minutes during which your strained features slowly relax, little by little, line by line, wrinkle by wrinkle, and at the end of the process you get to your feet, and you walk over to the phone, you pick up the phone book, you find the number to the closest police station, and you read the seven digits several times, a deep heaving sigh, your hand reaches for the telephone, your fingers touch it, and just then the phone rings, you give a start, pull your hand away, hesitate, then dare answer, Mélanie's voice, she wanted to know if you were still there, she's relieved to see you are, she tells you she'll be back very shortly, she's leaving in five minutes' time and she wants to be sure you'll wait for her, that you

– Wait for me, don't do anything that . . . Wait for me, Okay? Promise!

won't leave, you moisten your lips, you promise, she hangs up, as do you, your eyes on the police number, then you close the phone book, wander through the apartment, look at your surroundings, dirty dishes in the sink, you find some soap, wash all the dishes, your face impassive, then you resume walking around the apartment, the two framed pictures in the corner of the living room, you step closer, there's a hammer on the floor with two boxes of nails, a pencil, some duct tape, your face remains expressionless, but something flickers in your eye, a signal, permission, encouragement, so you take a frame, hold it against the wall at various heights, as though trying to visualize where it would look best, then you take the pencil, trace a mark on the wall, set the frame down, your face relaxed, the way it was when you used to putter around your house, in your other life, you open one of the two boxes of nails, but they're too small, you open the other box, the nails are much bigger, you choose one, pick up the hammer with your other hand and straighten up, you place the tip of the nail on the pencil mark, ready to hammer but you stop, your expression dissatisfied, as though the nails seemed too big now, you look to the floor then, no other nails, you walk to a cupboard, holding the hammer and the nail in the same hand, you open the cupboard, rummage inside with your free hand, find another box of nails, but they're as big as the one you have in your hand, you return to the living room, open the first drawer in the buffet, rummage through it with your free hand, nothing, second drawer, you come across a calendar open to the current month, you pick it up with your free hand, there's nothing but loose paper underneath, you cast a careless glance at the calendar before you go to close the drawer, then you frown, you lean over for a better look, a short newspaper clipping glued to the top of the page, a short text with three names that leap out at you, you pick up the calendar then, remove it from the drawer, the clipping is a funeral notice showing the names of your wife and your two children, the funeral home address, its business hours and viewing dates, February 25 and 26, and your lips open slowly, you squint uncomprehendingly, you examine the dates on the calendar page then, a few insignificant jottings on certain days, but there, on the small square for February 21, the date burned into your flesh, the day chaos reminded you who the true master is, on that date written in ink "High School Reunion," with an address and the name of a town, and I know what you're thinking as you recognize the name of the town, you're thinking it's not far from the place your family returned from that night, that the same route leads to both places, yes, the same road, and your eyes skip from the note in ink to the obituary, and you are no longer breathing, the sound of a door opening, closing, you turn your head, still not breathing, Mélanie stands there, Mélanie takes off her coat and lays it down on a chair, Mélanie says she was right, they're going to continue in spite of everything, in memory of Father Léo, because the burned body is most likely his, and she smiles in spite of it all, she draws near, but finally she sees the calendar in your left hand, she stops then, her smile evaporates then, she closes her eyes then, and everything comes to a standstill, and nothing happens for a long while, then she opens her eyes, looks you straight in the eye, walks toward you slowly, her voice calm and low, she had had too much to drink at the party, she'd been drinking too much for months to forget her futile and empty life, and she shouldn't have been driving, especially given the long road ahead of her, but she was so irresponsible, she took that damn curve too wide, too far outside, she failed to see the approaching vehicle, she failed even to see what became of it, of that car, she was too drunk and too happy that she'd missed it, just as she failed to glance back in her rearview mirror, at least she doesn't remember doing so, you have to believe her on that score, she insists, you have to, it was only the next day reading the newspaper that everything clicked, and then she panicked, then she fell apart and she didn't know what to do anymore, she thought of calling the police a thousand times, but she couldn't do it, she simply could not do it, she even seriously entertained the thought of killing herself, then after two days she remembered the group that she'd visited several times with little conviction, Father Léo's group, so that was where she went, like a lost child running toward the light, and this time everything was different, everything had changed, yes, everything, and as she speaks she draws closer to you, now she's right next to you, trembling with equal measures of distress and hope and you listen without moving a muscle, a wax figure posed in frozen abomination, and she continues speaking, she found the funeral home notice, she drove there, stayed in the background, and saw you, and since then she hasn't left you, followed you in her car when you fled from the funeral home, entered the bar Le Maquis shortly after you did, watched as you spoke to Sylvain, all the while wondering how she could approach you, because her decision had already been made, but in the end you were the one to approach her, because Father Léo was right, those who are suffering recognize each other, and you recognized her, consciously or unconsciously, you recognized her own suffering, she is sure of that, this she says three or four times, finally then you start to breathe again, a deep, painful, rasping breath, the calendar slips from your hand, the same hand that you lift to your eyes, the same eyes that you cover as you clench your teeth, the same teeth from which a hiss of the asphyxiated escapes, but Mélanie doesn't stop, her gentle hand on your cheek, the crack of her broken gaze and in her

– It was a sign, you've got to see that! A sign I could save you! And by saving you, I could save myself! We could save each other! Believe it! We can save each other! We've already started, I know it! And you know it too! We've started!

voice, you lower the hand covering your eyes then, your pupils flooded with black tears, your lips pulled back in a grimace of unspeakable suffering, your free hand steadily pushing Mélanie back to the wall beside the shelves, and she lets you, until her back is flat against the wall, and in her eyes misery and hope still coil around each other, into tragedy, into her voice more gentle than

– I already said it, I won't abandon you.

ever, your breathing rasping, your right hand still holding the hammer and nail, then your free hand picks up Mélanie's left wrist and slowly, ever so slowly, you lift it up and lay it flat against the wall, then you switch the nail to your other hand, place the tip of the nail against Mélanie's wrist, and she doesn't struggle, doesn't protest, just whispers that you can save each other, both of you, one saving the other, and slowly you lift the hammer, and the hiss that escapes through your lips is now one continuous moan, a moan becomes a sharp cry the moment the hammer hits the nail, and Mélanie scarcely reacts, a small gasp of pain, and your eyes still locked on hers, you swing again, four times, with each blow your frozen tears fall, and still Mélanie does not cry out, Mélanie whispers again and again that you both can, yes, you both can, you need to believe her, and when her left wrist is firmly fixed to the wall, you bend over painfully, water the floor with your tears, choose another large nail from the box, and you straighten up, and you take Mélanie's right wrist in your shaking hand, and you raise it to the wall at shoulder height, then you begin again, and this time your sobs tear at your throat, you're obliged to stop twice to wipe the mist from your eyes, while Mélanie recites in a calm but broken voice her desperate litany, finally, it's done, the hammer bounces off the floor, you take deep gasping breaths to choke back your tears, and Mélanie's voice, hovering, unearthly, refusing to stop, swearing the two of you can, you can, so you bend over, pick up the duct tape, tear off a wide strip that you smooth over Mélanie's lips, her voice smothered finally, you look at the woman crucified to the wall whose eyes never cease their pleading, you bring your face close to hers, and now you're no longer crying because your eyes are two craters erupting, desiccating forevermore any future tears, and the harsh caw of your voice rises from the bitterest of chasms, and your words

– *Live . . . and suffer.*

hit Mélanie full in the face, her eyes flood with despair then, finally you retreat, such tremendous heaviness, shouldering your coat, digging through Mélanie's coat, retrieving the keys to her car, you hear her calling in her voice muffled by the gag but you have no eyes for her, you leave the apartment, closing the door slowly behind you, and you take the stairs down, yes, down, to the street, and you return to the alley, and you find the trash can, and you dig out the gun, and you slide it into your coat pocket, return to the street, the sun blazing down, the street clear and bordered by huge banks of snow, you find Mélanie's car, you climb in and set off, you drive eyes straight ahead, take the south bridge out of the City, find yourself on a country road you've never travelled before, ninety minutes, the engine cuts out, no more gas, you have just enough time to pull over to the side of the road, then you step out and, without a glance back, you begin walking, along the road, along the deserted road that stretches into the countryside, your eyes an abyss tunnelled deeper with each step you take, and so you continue waging your war

against me

Author's Acknowledgements

Thank you to Karine Davidson-Tremblay, René Flageole, Alain Roy and Eric Tessier for their comments.

Thank you to Michel Vézina for the invitation.

Thank you to Sophie for everything.

Translators' Acknowledgements

Our thanks to Patrick Senécal, John Calabro and Beatriz Hausner. In memory of Katie Ouriou and Nora Alleyn.

Other books by Patrick Senécal

Sur le Seuil
Roman
Alire, 1998

Aliss
Roman
Alire, 2000

5150 rue des Ormes
Roman
Alire, 2002

Le Passager
Roman
Alire, 2003

Les 7 jours du Talion
Roman
Alire, 2002

Oniria
Roman
Alire, 2004

Le Vide
Roman
Alire, 2007

Sept comme Setteur
Roman pour la jeunesse
Éditions de la Bagnole, 2007

Hell.com
Roman
Alire, 2009

Madame Wenham
Roman pour la jeunesse
Éditions de la Bagnole, 2010

QUATTRO NOVELLAS

The Ballad of Martin B. by Michael Mirolla
Mahler's Lament by Deborah Kirshner
Surrender by Peter Learn
Constance, Across by Richard Cumyn
In the Mind's Eye by Barbara Ponomareff
The Panic Button by Koom Kankesan
Shrinking Violets by Heidi Greco
Grace by Vanessa Smith
Break Me by Tom Reynolds
Retina Green by Reinhard Filter
Gaze by Keith Cadieux
Tobacco Wars by Paul Seesequasis
The Sea by Amela Marin
Real Gone by Jim Christy
A Gardener on the Moon by Carole Giangrande
Good Evening, Central Laundromat by Jason Heroux
Of All the Ways To Die by Brenda Niskala
The Cousin by John Calabro
Harbour View by Binnie Brennan
The Extraordinary Event of Pia H. by Nicola Vulpe
A Pleasant Vertigo by Egidio Coccimiglio
Wit in Love by Sky Gilbert
The Adventures of Micah Mushmelon by Michael Wex
Room Tone by Gale Zoë Garnett